# A Season in Galicia

A story of gay love and romance in northern Spain

www.BarbarianSpy.com

This book is copyright © Shabbu (habu & Sabb)2016
habu and Sabb, writing as Shabbu, assert their right to be known as the author of this work.
Published by BarbarianSpy in 2016
Cover design © S Bush 2016
Cover image: Manipulated: All from Deposit Photos: Man
Copyright:prometeus, Grapes, Copyright:carballo
ISBN: 978-1-925568-00-4
All rights reserved

BarbarianSpy
Toronto, NSW
Australia

FOR LITERARY HEAT

# A Season in Galicia

A story of gay love and romance in northern Spain

by

## Shabbu

~

# Table of Contents

# Chapter One: Paul

The guitarist had been playing flamenco rhythms when I joined Ralph Peters, Sean Madden, and Holland Howard at one of the back tables in the Kennedy Center's small KC Jazz Club hall in Washington, D.C. I'd had a few stops to make after our practice of the Gay Men's Chorus of Washington at its P Street rehearsal hall just west of Dupont Circle. Ralph, who was a State Department cultural affairs officer—and a second tenor in the chorus—had invited us to come by to listen to a cultural exchange musician from Lugo, in Spain, he was herding around the country.

The tickets were free, I needed to stop in someplace warm anyway to get out of this damn interminable snowy winter weather on the East Coast that had intruded into spring, and I wasn't anxious to be at home this evening with Sean because we were in a rolling fight that I'd come to believe would lead to a termination of our relationship. I suddenly was glad that we hadn't tied the knot the first chance we'd gotten. I was willing; he less so. I guess he knew better than I did what real commitment required.

Sean was my last real tie to Washington—beyond the men's chorus, of course. And the young and twinky blond was that rare commodity, a first tenor, in the chorus. I was a much more plentiful baritone, so if one of us had to give that up to avoid the other, it really should be me. There wasn't much other reason to hang on. When I'd retired from the law practice early, at fifty-four, I'd said I wanted to travel the world footloose and free. But I hadn't taken my shoes from

7

under the bed Sean and I shared yet. I suspect he had been looking forward to me traveling the world too, so that he could put a variety of other shoes under my bed.

I was greeted at the Kennedy Center venue with relief by the second tenor, Ralph, who had the job of trying to make the room look like it was a sell-out crowd. I was waved in with obvious affection by Holland, who had been my colleague and mentor at the international law firm and who rounded out our little men's chorus quartet as a bass. And I was met frostily by Sean, who wanted me to know he was still in a snit, but who didn't want to push it too hard because I was the one keeping him in a luxury apartment just steps away, at the Watergate, and in food and clothes.

It took me some time to unravel all of the layers of clothing I had on in response to the snowfall outside that had continued into late March, and I had only started to complain about the weather when both Ralph and Howard held up their hands to stave off my now overly familiar complaint. I made no bones about preferring at least semitropical—or Mediterranean—climates. And yet I continued to live in the Mid-Atlantic states even past retirement and with a financial grounding that could permit me to live anywhere I wanted—and even to keep a tropical-climate second home. When I attempted the complaint, Sean just rolled his eyes and gave me a glassy stare.

The atmosphere with Sean became even more icy as the guitarist on stage segued into ballads and, for the first time, drew my attention. He was a handsome man, although perhaps with more character in his face than truly handsome. His features were rugged, dark, and brooding—almost sultry, I would say. His complexion was swarthy, with a two-day growth of beard that he probably kept at that length for the macho effect. I gauged him to be in his late twenties or early thirties. His raven-black hair was wavy and worn long, shoulder length. He was slim, nearly to the point of being gaunt, but he also was muscular. I knew from the program provided that he was Spanish, from Galicia, the northwest quadrant of the country, famous for its vineyards, and I could see him spending as much time working in the vineyard as at his musical craft. He was a strange mix of refinement and roughness, and I was drawn to him by more than his music.

That wasn't to say that he wasn't proficient enough at his musical craft to be sponsored for a trip to the States and small-venue concerts in rooms like this one at the Kennedy Center. The spotlight was on the strong, calloused hands, with the long, sensuous fingers, that he was using to play his guitar, and it was as much that as the beauty I found in him and the sweet ballad music he was playing that captivated my attention—and, yes, my arousal.

The Galicia region of Spain, I thought. I hadn't considered going there. I had considered Portugal, though, which also was on the Atlantic coast just south of Galicia. I decided I would consider that part of Spain now, especially after I'd leaned over to Ralph and said, "Are all the men in Galicia that sexy?"

"All of them under forty," Ralph had answered, with a laugh.

I looked over at Sean, who was pouting, which, of course, on his Byronesque blond visage, looked cute, and I realized that it was, indeed, over with him. I no longer was that interested in "cute"—and certainly not in brooding.

I had retired in a pique. It wasn't Howard who had asked me if my coming out would hurt the business of the law firm, but it might as well have been him. He knew I was gay. He had initiated me—years and years ago when I was clerking for him. But he wasn't surfacing this question among the other senior partners of the firm. He was too powerful. They only brought it up when I paraded Sean out and joined the gay men's chorus. Howard hadn't come out; I had. And it wasn't Howard who took the consequences.

So, I retired early; took my assets, which were considerable, out of the firm; and started a new, carefree life. But had I really? Was I really carefree? I was still here in

9

Washington, still with Sean in my bed—but not enjoying that nearly as much as I had when it was all hush hush.

"And what do you think of our Spanish guitarist? I mean his music, not his sultry beauty," Ralph whispered to me while the musician was taking a short break. Ralph was the nervous type, and for some reason he always wanted to know what I thought about one of his State Department cultural projects. Maybe he kept asking because I was always honest with him and he often made adjustments from my suggestions.

"He's beautiful," I answered. "I'd like to take him home with me."

"I meant the music, I said," Ralph shot back, with a laugh. "You're always ready to take a good-looking man home."

I heard a huff from the other side of the table. I thought that Ralph and I were conversing at low enough volume, but perhaps not. That was at the base of our rolling fight. Sean had dragged me to an art gallery opening—he was a curator at the Smithsonian—and had left me to flutter around with a group of his friends, so I'd taken one of the artists home for the night. Sean somehow had expected me to just stand around and be his presentable meal ticket, I guess. But if he thought I was going to let him control me like that simply because I was moving up in age, he was sadly mistaken.

Besides, I'd taken the artist home because I sensed that Sean was going to go off with one of his friends. And, indeed, he didn't return home that night. I had done what I did, I now thought, to bring the roundabout arguing we'd been doing to a boil.

"The music is beautiful too," I said. "I very much like how his hands were spotlighted. I suggest you keep that in future concerts."

"Will do. Thanks. I'm glad you liked that. I'm taking him to Vinoteca for a late dinner, and he's agreed to play a few sets in their upstairs lounge. Would you like to go with us?"

"Yes," I shot back immediately.

"And would Sean—?"

"No. We drove separately, and I know Sean has an exhibit to put together and needs to be at work early tomorrow. We'll just not mention Vinoteca, shall we?"

Vinoteca was a small, exclusive restaurant in northwest D.C. that included trendy jazz and specialty music in its upstairs lounge. Ralph often took the exchange musicians there for more intimate gigs.

It was in the upstairs lounge at Vinoteca that I learned that the Spanish guitarist, who Ralph introduced me to as Xavier Franco and who had a firm handshake and a divine, speculative smile, also had a heavenly tenor voice and I became totally smitten with the man.

And if I had to guess, I would have said he was smitten with me too. We sat near him at a table, and all the time he was playing and singing, he seemed to be playing just for me—to me. When he'd asked how I liked his concert at the Kennedy Center, I had been honest—that the flamenco music very good, but what really caught my interest were the ballads. And here, at Vinoteca, he played mostly ballads. He played them and he sang them to me.

He started off one by explaining that it was an Irish Celtic song but that his region of Spain had once been Celtic too and retained the influence of the Celts in its music. Thus, he was going to sing "Star of County Down," which I joined in applauding as I knew that ballad well—we'd sung it in the gay men's chorus—but he was going to alternate the verses in the languages of his home—Galego, Castilian, and the musical-heritage Celtic language. He would sing the chorus in English.

Somehow Ralph must have told him I sang too and knew that ballad, because when he came to the first singing of the chorus, he paused and motioned to me.

11

"From Bantry Bay up to Derry quay and from Galway to Dublin town . . ." he sang in a clear, high tenor. On the next line, "No maid I've seen like the brown colleen that I met in the County Down," I tentatively came in under him in a baritone harmony with the melody he was singing.

I came in stronger on the next chorus, after he'd sung verse two: "As she onward sped . . ." in Castilian Spanish, and here, as he guided me, I took over the melody of the chorus, with him soaring above me in a tenor harmony.

I was smitten, and the decibel rating of the applause indicated that others had been smitten too.

A beaming Ralph put his hand on my forearm amid the hearty applause and said, "I have Xavier booked into the Georgetown Suites Harbor Hotel, which should be on your way home to the Watergate. It's getting very late and I have to check in at State before I go home—and Randy's been complaining a lot lately on how late I've been getting home. Would you mind terribly . . . ?"

No, I wouldn't mind at all.

\* \* \* \*

I'm sure we both knew we were going to fuck when Xavier took my car keys from me, handed them over to the valet, and invited me up to his hotel room. But it was still a surprise to me that, when I came up to his room from the bar downstairs with the bottle of whiskey he wanted and two glasses, I found him stripped down to his briefs and sitting on the side of the bed, strumming his guitar.

He spoke better English than I spoke Spanish, so that's what we spoke. I was impressed that although he had all of the rugged looks of a farm laborer—belied as they were by the sensitive way he stroked his guitar strings—he spoke so many languages, as he had demonstrated by singing in Spanish and Galician as well as Celtic and English. And I was nonplused that we did talk, sitting there side by side on the hotel bed, sipping whiskey, and talking about Spain and music and his impressions of the States, when we both knew what we were working up to, especially since he settled that off the top.

"Ralph told me he knows you from some sort of gay men's choir—that you both go with men."

"That's right," I answered. "Does that make you uncomfortable?"

"No, not in the least. I find you very attractive. Ralph tells me that you are very well equipped, as well."

"Does he now?"

"He says you are a top."

"Mostly. I have gone both ways, but, yes, I prefer to top. I hope that—"

"Is convenient? Yes it is. I knew as soon as I saw you that we were going to fuck. I do like to have some form of release after playing concerts as tonight. That cultural palace on the river is quite intimidating to someone who comes from rural Galicia."

"Cultural palace on the river? Oh, you mean the Kennedy Center. Yes, it's imposing, I suppose, but we have arts centers like that in most of our big cities. I thought the jazz club setting was just right for your performance. It was very intimate—sensual even—and I thought it suited you. You're a very sexy young man, you know."

I was confused. I was used to working up to it. He had initially been very direct—and matter of fact. It was as if having established we would fuck—and, indeed, I could see that he was as hard inside his briefs as I knew I was—he now wanted to revert to some cultural form of foreplay.

We had spoken of getting it on—making sure we were a fit, which, I was pleased to learn, we were. But he now was talking of his experiences on his tour. I almost laughed. I was sitting beside him, still fully clothed, the two of us nursing a bottle of whiskey, and nearly nude he had approached getting down to the sex I assumed we would have—we both knew I could tell he was hard; I certainly

13

was—and were now having a civil conversation on his impressions of his musical program.

"I have played in Madrid and Barcelona, of course. They are more festive than here. They chatter through the music, but somehow still absorb it completely. The audiences I've played to here so far are so serious. I wonder if they really like—"

"Your audiences at both the Kennedy Center and the restaurant this evening were mesmerized by your playing, Xavier. You understand what mesmerized means?"

Xavier nodded that he did. I continued. "They listened so silently out of respect and because they didn't want to miss a single chord of what you were playing or lose the tune of what you were singing. You didn't like this reaction?"

"No, I did like that I wasn't just background music. But it put so much responsibility on me—I felt like I had to work so much harder to make it sound right. I'm afraid I made many mistakes. In Spain, I play at the outdoor restaurants at night and just sit in the shadows, giving a foundation to the dinner conversation."

"You made no mistakes that I or, I'm sure, anyone else heard, Xavier. Your playing was divine. And you know what else is divine?"

"No, what?"

"Your body is divine. The curve of your hard cock that I'm tracing inside your briefs is divine. And the whiskey bottle is empty. And it's getting late. I want to make love to you now."

"No, I wish to make love to your body first," he said, as he laid his guitar aside, sank to his knees in front of me, gently parted my knees to put my legs into a wide-open stance, unzipped my trousers, fished my cock out, and opened his lips over it. As I sighed and leaned back, burying my elbows into the surface of the bedspread behind me, he moved a hand up my belly to my chest, opening buttons on my shirt and spreading the shirt open as he moved.

14

The abruptness and baldness with which he went about it embarrassed me and actually made me start to go soft, so I pulled him up to beside me on the bed, embraced him with one arm, and my hand went to his dick through the material of his briefs as his hand encased my cock. I moved us back to panting foreplay. That helped return me to getting hard and I was able to get him going in that direction too. I tried to kiss him on the lips, but he turned his face from me. It was obvious he wasn't interested in that sort of intimacy. He did, however allow me to kiss him elsewhere on the face, in the hollow of his neck, and down to his nipples.

He came quickly with just that much attention. I had managed to move my hand under the waistband of his briefs and grasp and stroke his cock a few times before he came, but not much more. It was as if he hadn't really done this before and had no control over building up his arousal.

After he came, he pushed me off him, stood and stripped his briefs off, mounted the bed, and immediately went on all fours, with his legs spread and his tail turned to me. He was signaling that he wanted to get on with it—that he was offering his ass for me.

It was a very nice ass. His thighs and buttocks were covered with a curly black down and even his asshole was rimmed with black fuzz. Aroused by his lean, sinewy body, much more of the man of the outdoors and hard work than I was used to encountering in the cultural circles I traveled in, I moved behind him, working my tongue over the down on his thighs and buttocks and then smoothing down that encircling his rim before moving my tongue inside him. I grasped his cock, pulled it back between his legs, and divided my efforts and attention between his asshole and his cock and balls.

He moaned, trembled, and moved languidly under my embrace. It took time for me to open him to the point that I thought he could take me and then more time, with him grunting and groaning but holding in place like a bitch dog wanting it, before I could finally work my thickness inside.

But then he just stoically took it until I had pumped him to an ejaculation.

Afterward, we stretched out against each other on the bed, naked, and he let me embrace him and slow stroke his cock as we both dozed off. I made another move to kiss him on the lips, but this obviously wasn't something he liked, so I desisted. He still left me with the impression—even though there was no holding back from him in letting me fuck him—that he hadn't been with that many men before.

When I woke sometime in the middle of the night, it was with an aching pain in the arm that I had under him, encasing his waist at this point. His back was propped up on pillows against the headboard, and he was smoking a cigarette, a little frown on his face, his face highlighted by the only illumination in the room, the lamp on the nightstand.

"Do you regret—?" I started to say, but he didn't let me finish the sentence.

"No, of course not."

I moved my left arm from under him while moving my right arm over his belly and turning toward him. I lowered my mouth to his right nipple and licked and sucked it. He was breathing more heavily than when I woke and I could feel his dick start to harden under the attentions of my right hand. But his cigarette apparently was important enough to him not to respond otherwise.

"I don't think you're supposed to be smoking in this hotel," I murmured, "especially not in bed."

"If they want to chase me down for it, they'll have to follow me to Spain," he said, his voice a low growl—not angry, more disinterested in what anyone thought about him smoking.

"So, even from what you've seen in the States, you want to go back to Spain?" It was a pertinent question. He looked like he came from rough, somewhat primitive circumstances in Spain—although I'll have to admit that this was a large part of his turn-on factor for me—and from what I heard from Ralph on these cultural exchange programs, it

16

was a problem often to return musicians like him to their home circumstances after they'd gotten a taste of the amenities and appreciative paying audiences in the States. The program was meant to seed pro-American sentiment in countries abroad, not to skim off the cultural cream of other societies, but often the effect was the latter.

"I can't wait to go home. I am enjoying this tour, yes, but I would wither and die if I was away from Galicia for long. That is heaven on earth."

He spent considerable time then, as I was working his nipple with my mouth and his cock with my hand telling me of how much a paradise that region of Spain was. And, though I was concentrating in preparing him for sex again, I was listening to him too, and he had me convinced of the glories of the region he came from.

My preparation had a surprising end though—one I didn't take into consideration and never would have thought I would enjoy, but that made me lost to him. His cigarette and sales job on Galicia finished, he stubbed the butt out on the corner of the nightstand—which I'm sure was viewed with alarm the next day by the hotel maid—reversed himself on me and stretched over me. We sixty-nined for several minutes until—and past the time that—I was craving release, Xavier refusing to stop working me when I said I was ready to come.

When I did come, spouting off on his throat and chest, and was then in a moment of weakness and vulnerability, he quickly moved off me, reversed his body again, and turned me belly to bed. Slipping his arms under my arm pits, he put me in a full Nelson, arched my torso off the surface of the bed, and, as I screamed bloody loud in surprise and initial pain, he skewered me to great depth with his long, thin, hard cock, and pumped me hard and fast to his own ejaculation. Only as he came, did I realize he wasn't sheathed. I had been fucked before but not for some time— and certainly bareback. He wasn't thick, but he was long and a total surprise—not only that he'd do it but also that he'd do

17

it with such cruel, powerful thrusts. Shocking as it was, it totally aroused me, and I came again before he did.

Without a word, he rolled off me, turned out the light on the nightstand, and was snoring within minutes. I took that as a signal that we were to sleep then. It might have been a signal for me to leave him and go home, but I found I didn't want to. He was such a change for me, had such an arousing body, gave me something I hadn't had for some time—excitement, surprise, and variety.

He also had fucked me; I had forgotten that I once could be satisfactorily completed with a man inside me. And what a man he was.

I was disconcerted and slightly unfulfilled by his complete noninterest in kissing or exploring each other's bodies with hands and tongues. I never quite reached satisfactory intimacy with him either that night or later. But it occurred to me that this was part of the heightened arousal with him—continually wanting more—and that perhaps what took me to higher levels of arousal and prolonged the mystery of having sex with him rather than Sean, who was all touchy feely, was the raw lust he evoked, stripped of any attempts at affection.

I was awakened by the sound of the telephone ringing on the nightstand next to Xavier. Drapes were pulled over the window, but the sunlight that was fighting to get into the room at the edges of the window and at the slit where the drapes were pulled together told me that it was way past dawn. Still early for me. Since I'd retired, I'd gotten up when I woke up—which was usually a lot closer to noon than to dawn.

Xavier was laying beside me, on his back, propped up against the headboard, and smoking another cigarette. He picked up the phone and then handed it over to me. "It's for you," he said.

"For me?" Who the fuck knew I was here, in Xavier's hotel room? I hadn't even known I'd be here this morning. It was Ralph Peters.

"Paul," I heard him say. "I trust you had an interesting night."

"You could say so," I answered. "How the fuck did you—?"

"I hope Xavier was satisfactory."

"One hell of a surprise," I answered. "But how the fuck did—?"

"Listen, I'm in a bind, and you're retired. And if you are hitting it off with Xavier and all, I was wondering . . . and you have been saying that you were antsy in retirement and were looking for a little excitement. Well, I was wondering. Xavier's on a three-week tour. Chicago from here and then San Francisco and L.A. Back to Austin and then Atlanta before going back to Spain. I'm really swamped here. I'm wondering if you'll travel with him. Be his handler for State. I know I can get it approved. All expenses paid."

"Me, travel around the country with Xavier? I don't know how I can . . . or if he'd want to . . ."

I had to take a breath. Xavier had smiled and wagged his head to signal he was happy with that and then had leaned over my body and taken my cock in his mouth to seal his approval.

"You don't have that many responsibilities here," Ralph said. "We both know that. And I know you're writing gay novels now, but you can do that anywhere—and I think that Xavier could give you a plotline to purse anyway. Besides, it's been a hard winter here in D.C. and you've made it harder by continuously complaining of the cold and the snow. Granted Chicago will be colder, but the rest of the trip will be in warmer climes, and we'll surely be having springtime weather by the time you return to D.C."

I couldn't argue with that. And so I didn't, arranging to visit him in State later in the afternoon to start the process of taking over from him as Xavier's handler on this tour.

Handler. Which was rather funny, because Xavier was working on giving me a blow job and was handling my ass with a finger stroking my prostate when I placed the receiver back on the telephone.

"I'm glad you will be my guide," Xavier said, with a deep growl in his voice. "Now I want to fuck. But who takes who first?" I opted to side-split him languidly for starters and I ended up with my shoulders bearing my weight on the hotel room carpet next to the bed and him standing and holding my legs spread wide in the air as he jackhammered down into my ass.

There was more of the same as we traveled around the States. As he practiced in the afternoons, I wrote to a novel draft inspired by our arrangement. The novel was finished and snarfed up by my publisher before we reached Atlanta. I would accompany him to his concerts in the evenings, doing all of the managerial work, and then we'd flip-flop fuck much of the night away in hotel rooms— leaving a swath of first-class hotels with burn marks on the corners of the nightstands all across the country. Most of the mornings were for sleeping to recover from exhaustion and more sex to recover a modicum of exhaustion.

By the time we reached Hartsfield-Jackson Atlanta International Airport in Atlanta and I was waving him toward the departure ramp, I was smitten, totally adjusted to an exciting new life that I knew now would be cut off in an instant, and was ruminating over what I could do to keep the wet dream from ending.

The stake of this was driven through my heart and I was spurred to unthinking action when I arrived back in Washington, D.C., to find that Sean had cleared out of my apartment in the Watergate and was now living with Ralph Peters, displacing the last man he had in his bed, Randy, apparently. It was like musical beds in Ralph's place.

I didn't discover they were now a pair until I went to the next practice of the gay men's chorus and found them wrapped up in each other. It took Howard to explain the obvious to me. Ralph had used the time that I was floating around the States doing his job to take Sean from me. It

20

didn't matter that before I left I was trying to think of ways to pry Sean out of my bed. I certainly didn't want it to be a matter of someone taking him away from me.

My ego bruised, and seeing myself as a laughingstock, I skipped the next men's chorus practice, not wanting to come face to face with the pair. The day after I'd done that, I realized that there really wasn't anything keeping me tied to my current location and life at all. And I was finding myself dreaming of Xavier and missing his shocking and surprising ways.

Focused, off kilter, and completely frustrated, I went on the Internet and began researching houses in the Lugo region of Spain's Galicia—where Xavier was from. Xavier hadn't given me his address—in truth he hadn't given me any means of contacting him, although, as I now remembered it, I'd tried to get that from him—until I realized he didn't have to tell me. All of his contact information in Spain was in the paperwork I held as we traveled around the States on his cultural tour.

He came from a village called Guntin to the southwest of the larger town of Lugo. Within forty-eight hours of looking, I'd contracted and sent a deposit on a partially renovated nineteenth-century stone country villa outside of the village of Friol, twenty-two kilometers northwest of Lugo.

I had tasted the surprise and variety of Xavier—and of the flip-flop, which I'd had no idea would send me so far up into the clouds of arousal and completion. There was nothing to hold me in Washington, D.C.—or in the States, for that matter. I was going off for an adventure in retirement and for rejuvenation in rural Spain.

# Chapter Two: Alex

Edward Michaels had been the last of a now-extinct breed, I thought, as I left the Spanish churchyard after his interment.

I missed him badly. Always well dressed, polite, and well mannered, he had been quietly confident of his own worth and had always avoided publicity and the bright lights. A true English gentleman of the old kind, I had always thought. And in our own way, we had been lovers. In recent months he had behaved publicly as if I were his partner and we had married weeks before he died. We had done this more for the legal protection it gave me than because we needed to. And now he was gone I was the owner of Pazo Carbello, a large old stone manor house in Galicia that was still in need of work, along with rather extensive fincas, or vineyards. The last two years had seen those extended and revitalized but there was more work to do.

I had met Edward when I first arrived in England from Australia. Having admired his writing greatly, I had written to him, through his publisher, telling him how much I enjoyed his humor and wit and his writing, and that I was coming to England in a few months and would like to buy him lunch. I had received a polite reply inviting me to get in touch closer to my arrival. I had. I was excited at the possible opportunity to meet one of my favorite authors face to face.

He chose the restaurant, of course, the Rio Mino. It was in a village outside London that took me a morning train trip to reach, and it was a long walk to get to the restaurant. He had parked his old Rolls Royce in front of it when he arrived as if it were in his private parking place. I was amused by the car and impressed by him, dressed smartly in a navy pinstripe suit that fit his lean frame perfectly and was obviously expensive. He was polite and the conversation was engrossing and easy. It was quickly obvious that we had common interests and tastes. We laughed honestly at each other's jokes but were both serious about other things and shared a love of nature. He was over thirty years older than I was.

At the end of lunch he asked me if I was looking for work as he was considering employing a new secretary, or "office person/dogsbody," as he put it, for a few months. I said "yes." I had come to England for a short break to see some relatives and immerse myself in some history. I was a writer too, but a not very successful one, and was hoping a holiday, a break away from the routine of working and writing, might provide inspiration for a more successful book. An extended paid holiday in England working for Edward was a golden opportunity for me. He assured me I'd have plenty of free time to write if I took the job, but I'd have taken it anyway.

We met again the next day. The local cab driver picked me up from the village inn where I had spent the night and took me to Edward's house. It was a beautiful large, two-story, seventeenth-century country house with four big diamond-paned windows at the front surrounded by ivy-coated stone walls. It was the sort of house tourists all want to see when they go to the English countryside and the sort people dream of living in.

Edward's previous secretary, Mrs. Carter, had retired a few months before and he had not got around to replacing her. Now he wanted his business papers and library organized so he could go away for a while. Exactly where and why he was vague about. He said it could be a live-in position if that suited me. Because of the location of his house—it was some distance from the village railway station—it was not a place you could commute to from London. Mrs. Carter had lived in the next village. He recommended I get a cheap car if I took the job or I would be rather isolated there. The salary was small, but it included room and board, and I accepted his offer without hesitation. We agreed I'd start the following Monday morning and the cab would meet me at the station at 10:00 a.m.

Edward was from a well-connected family, his mother had been the niece of an English duke, though the details about his father and early life in his online biographies were vague. I had thought from his writing that he was probably gay but knew he had been married. A possible relationship had not been my motivation in wanting to meet him, and I had been relieved that he had not invited me to his house the first night to discuss the job he was offering.

I found the work was a great education in what even a moderately successful author has to deal with. Agents, publishers, fan mail, and taxes, all the paperwork came past me, beginning with a pile of similar correspondence that had been accumulating since Mrs. Carter left.

I quickly discovered that Edward was selling his house. I was shocked and asked him why. "It's too much to keep up at my age," he replied. Having seen some of his finances by then, I understood that he meant it cost too much. His income was not large and he lived well.

"Where will you be going?" I asked, feeling sad that he would have to leave it and also sorry that my position would only be for a short time.

"That, Alex, is a question I am still considering. Will I stay here in this part of England or return to the place where I was born, on the river Mino?" he replied, giving me a small smile.

I assumed he had been born in England and the river Mino meant nothing to me. It was only a month before we left England that I finally discovered where he had decided to go. To Spain. He never seemed secretive about it, though, just very private in some ways.

When we left England we had been lovers for a couple of months. It was not a deliberate or gradual thing; it was something that happened suddenly.

We'd sometimes spend the evenings together, sharing dinner and then watching TV, and it was on one of those nights that my suspicions about Edward's sexuality were unexpectedly confirmed.

The movie we were watching was deeply moving, *A Single Man*, about a gay man who loses his partner suddenly in an auto accident and doesn't feel it's worth living anymore. I was in tears at the end, embarrassed at my emotional display, and worried what Edward might think of me.

But Edward put an arm around my shoulders and pulled me to him, saying, "It's only a film." We held there, me liking the comfort, wondering if I would ever find a special partner as the protagonist in the film had and how it would be if he died. Wondering if finding someone was worth the pain of losing them. Also feeling myself aroused by the physical contact.

"It's only a film, Alex. And life is too good to give it away before you have to."

I looked up into his eyes and saw they were looking at me in a certain way and his eyes were damp too. I kissed him on the lips. He returned the kiss and pulled me closer. We stayed there for some time, kissing, then stroking each other, his hand moving under the waistband of the tracksuit pants I had on. Moving to my stiffening cock and caressing it. I am sure he stroked me first, but my hand moved to feel his package soon after. Discovering that his reaction to being touched was positive, I became more aroused, a thrill going through me at knowing I aroused him.

"This would be more comfortable in bed, if you want . . ." he said.

I have no idea what I replied but we went up to his room together. The idea of Edward stripping off his clothes and having sex on the couch was shocking.

* * * *

Edward eventually informed me that he was going to Spain. It was not a surprising destination for an older Englishman to retire to.

"Warmer weather," I replied, "and more economical."

"Not warmer, actually," he said with a small smile. "And if you don't mind the cold, I'd like you to come with me."

I was surprised and elated. I had been trying not to think of losing him and felt a flood of relief. I barely heard his remark about the cold or thought of his earlier one about returning where he had been born.

After I had been working for him for six months, Edward and I went to Spain. The house in England had been sold for a very large sum. It was a beautiful house a reasonable distance from London by train. From the papers I saw mentioning the sale, a large part of the proceeds had gone to settle debts, but that still left a sizeable sum. For some years Edward had lived well, but beyond his means, as they used to say. The royalties that came in from his books had once been sufficient to buy the house and restore it and maintain his lifestyle, and more, but there had been an expensive divorce, I gathered, and his royalties had shrunk considerably in recent years.

The publishing game had got tougher and money tighter, he was no longer a fashionable author, and there hadn't been a new book of his released for nearly eight years. I knew he had one he was working on, though.

We took several days to drive to Spain in the Rolls Royce—an elegant way to enter a land full of past glories and history—and arrived at a sprawling old stone manor house in the far northwest of the country, near the river Mino. After leaving a modern highway it seemed we had also left the modern world, going down a very narrow bitumen road past an ancient, high granite stone wall before turning into open iron gates. Ahead of us was a short, white graveled driveway running between tall poplars, leading us to huge metal studded wooden doors that stood open to reveal a flight of stone steps. It was like entering a castle.

This was not the Spain I had imagined. There were no white bungalows, no flat plains, or dry earth, or sun-drenched beaches. Instead, there was an ancient granite manor house, lush greenery, rugged mountains full of vineyards, small villages with dark granite stone houses, and spectacular scenery. It was also quite cold.

The interior of the manor house had been updated and well furnished forty or fifty years before. It had a large bathroom that worked and a traditional hooded fireplace in the kitchen, as well as a wood cooking stove and a gas one. There was a stone-hooded fireplace in the main living room, or salon, as the Spanish called it. There were eight bedrooms, mostly small, a large dining room, a small dining room and a library as well as a second, small salon. That was upstairs, reached by a large enclosed staircase with doors at the bottom that could be shut to seal it off from the lower floor. Downstairs were unused animal pens, servant's rooms and kitchens, a wine cellar, and a garage. Nearby was a large slate-roofed stone barn containing bales of hay, a tractor, and a variety of farm equipment. I later found that in the vineyards there was another barn that was a bodega, or wine cellar. About the estate there were also the ruins of an abandoned barn and a servants' house.

Needless to say, this was not what I had expected when Edward told me we were going to a house he had in Spain.

I had expected the Costa Del Sol, sun, warmth, a comfortable large house or a small villa by the sea. Not the north of Spain, a wild landscape of hills and narrow roads, on which deer were often seen. A place where wild boar still

27

roamed the hills, and possibly wolves. Wild horses were to be found further to the north, I was told.

Within fifteen minutes of our arrival, several cars had driven up the driveway and parked in the courtyard of the house, and a gaggle of mostly elderly Spaniards bearing food and wine had arrived to welcome Edward. I was introduced as his secretary. I had absolutely no Spanish, unlike Edward, who obviously was fluent in it, and ate, drank, and nodded my way through most of the party before quietly disappearing into what I was sure was my bedroom, as it had my suitcase in it and some boxes of things that had been sent ahead from England. I slept and dreamed and had a generally restless night. There was obviously far more to Edward than I, or the public, knew. I wondered if his name really was Edward Michaels but remembered that was what his passport and business papers said. I realized he could easily have changed it legally, though, in his younger days.

I only now was beginning to understand that Edward had his feet in two separate worlds. Knowing more of the Spanish connection explained much of the tension of place that I'd read in his novels.

In the morning I asked him what his Spanish connection was, and he replied, "It's very complicated, and nothing to concern yourself with, Alex." His evasiveness only made me more curious.

Life was very different in Spain, but also not different. Work was started immediately on making several bedrooms larger, with their own bathrooms, and installing central heating. Instead of Agnes arriving at 9:00 a.m. to clean and cook for us, it was now Maria. And a man called Pepe came and worked on the surrounding vineyards, with his son, Jacobo. Edward would go out now and then to see what they were doing, and after several weeks invited me to go with him.

"Would you like to learn how a vineyard works, Alex?" he asked me when we returned from what had been an extensive tour of the estate with Pepe.

I had found it fascinating and had asked questions about everything: the age of the vines, the way they were trained on the wires, the types of grapes they were growing. The tour ended with a tasting in the stone bodega on the other side of the vineyards from the house of some of the wines Pepe had made. The wines were light, easy-drinking wines that reminded me of rosés. Edward had to answer my questions or translate them for Pepe or Jacobo to answer and translate the answers back to me. I wished I had enough Spanish to understand Pepe's and Jacobo's answers myself.

At the end of the tour Edward looked exhausted.

I answered his question with a, "Yes, I'd like that," of course. But I had no idea why he wanted me to learn about the vineyards, as he was quite capable of managing them himself with Pepe's help. And Pepe and his son had obviously been managing them while Edward was in England.

But I was interested, and it was good to have an excuse to get out of the house and into the fresh air and sunshine.

I had been extremely busy since we arrived reworking the first two of Edward's books for publication as e-books. A letter to his publisher had confirmed Edward still held the digital rights to his fourteen published novels, and the publisher's offer for those rights was not what I felt they were worth. I had put the proposal to him to self-publish the first two to see how they went. I set out what I thought were the pros and cons of going it alone with digital publication, and Edward had agreed to me setting them up for publishing with online outlets such as Amazon's Kindle store. If it didn't work out, he could take them down and instead take what the publisher was offering him for the rights to all his novels.

In the vineyard I got a break from the computer, and it was not only fresh air that revived me but also being with two good-looking men, one older and one younger than me. I thought Pepe had perhaps looked at me as if he had some

29

interest. But I knew he and his son were both married and it was a small place where everyone obviously knew everyone else and everyone's business. It was also a complicated situation with Edward employing us all and the relationship Edward and I had, and I had no intention of causing any problems, or of betraying Edward.

An old man called Antonio came to the house regularly also. He worked in the flower and vegetable gardens and the orchard when he was not sitting on the terrace at the back of the house drinking wine with Edward.

I had discovered that Edward was fluent in Spanish the first day we arrived, and, as I wanted to learn Spanish as fast as I could, I went off to a teacher in Monforte de Lemos for lessons two mornings a week. With my regular work, the e-books, the vineyards, and Spanish lessons, I was busy all day every day.

* * * *

"It's time," I said to Edward, and he sat down to look at the computer screen over my shoulder.

It had taken nearly three months for me to get his first two novels set up for publication, or uploading. Covers had been specially made that were reminiscent of the originals. We were not able to use the original artwork because the publisher had wanted a fortune for the rights.

Edward watched intently as I uploaded the first one. "I can't believe publishing has gone this far in the last ten years," he said. "When I think of what it took to get a book out when I began writing thirty years ago and what you have done. . . ."

"You need to finish the book you are working on," I said.

"Perhaps," he replied.

When I was done with the first book we both looked at the page showing it for sale. "That is it? Some time on a computer and pushing a few buttons, and voila, I am on sale to the world. It doesn't seem real. Where are the months of review and preparation, the meetings with editors and publicists?"

"These books had been through all that already," I reminded him. "We weren't starting from scratch with them." He was partly right, though, we had paid an editor, who had done a professional edit of what had already been fully edited books, and had a cover designer make the cover. But there were no other professionals involved. For these digital books there was not even a book designer, and certainly no publicist.

Edward was well known enough that we didn't think it would be worth the expense.

Edward put an arm about my neck, pulling my head back and kissing the top of it. "Whether this works or not, thank you, Alex. It has been a very interesting experience."

He sat there as I published the second book. Then we kissed and went up to his bedroom. It was a fitting way to celebrate the event. Later I uploaded the two books to several other Internet bookstores.

* * * *

"I heard that Monica has some puppies for sale, and, as we needed a dog to replace Tibouchi, I have bought one of them. Monica calls her Angel, but I am sure you will come up with a better name for her. And she will give you a hobby."

Edward had said this in an offhand way when we were starting lunch. When he was offhand it always seemed to mean that something was more serious than he made it sound and I wondered what could be the hidden meaning in getting a new dog.

Tibouchi had been the farm dog when we arrived. Supposedly a guard dog, he was big, but so old he was gray all over and half blind. He spent his days following the sun around the farmhouse, flopping first in one spot and then, when the shadows arrived, moving to another, sunnier one. One day we saw that the shadows had covered him, and we knew, without even touching him, that he had gone. Pepe buried him at the end of one of the rows of vines near the house. Now the place seemed lonely without him always outside.

"It will be good to have another dog, but I am not sure how a puppy will give me a hobby," I replied. "Apart from taking him for walks."

"It is a purebred dog, Alex, an English Cocker Spaniel, and Monica would like her shown and will take you both to some dog shows and teach you what to do."

I was sure there was more to it than Edward was saying, but he often kept things back, and he usually knew what I would like. I did like the idea of getting off the farm now and then and meeting more people. Spanish lessons and an occasional trip to the swimming pool or gym were not getting me a lot of friends, mainly because I couldn't speak enough Spanish yet to hold even a simple conversation. I had asked Edward to speak Spanish with me, to help me learn, but he was reluctant to do so.

"I like to speak English, Alex, and you are the only one here I can speak good English with," he had replied.

All I could say was, "I understand." The people who visited the farm who spoke English didn't speak much of it; their conversations with Edward rapidly moved into Spanish.

Pepe spoke some English, but only what related to the work in the vineyard and the winemaking, so our conversations were limited. I was rapidly learning to follow that limited Spanish, but it didn't give me the vocabulary I needed for socializing.

A few weeks after getting the puppy I went to my first dog show with Monica. It was in Lugo, a two-hour drive away from the farmhouse, and I was gone for the whole day. It felt strange being separated from Edward for so long, but I had enjoyed it. Especially as I met several English speakers there, mainly English people, who I could hold a conversation with. My Spanish also benefited, as Monica was very social and there always was someone coming up to speak to her in Spanish. My puppy didn't win anything. That was my only disappointment for the day, as I thought she was beautiful and the best one there. I called her Cocky in private. It described her perfectly, but I kept to Angel in front of Monica.

Spanish farm dogs were usually outside dogs, as Tibouchi had been. But Edward had relented and let Cocky come into the house at night. I had told him I was worried she would be too cold and lonely in the barn on her own. But she was not allowed in my bedroom. Edward didn't approve of a dog on the bed, and there were times he came to my bedroom at night, so I didn't argue with him. I had instead made her a very warm bed in the hallway next to a central-heating radiator.

\* \* \* \*

"How much money do you have, Alex?" Edward asked. He had been out all morning and asked the question as he walked into the room I used as an office.

"I have a few hundred in cash here," I said, opening the bottom desk drawer and taking out the cash box. "How much do you need?"

"No. That is not what I mean. How much money do you have personally, Alex, in the bank, in stocks? Whatever it is you have your savings invested in."

"I suppose I could get $15,000," I replied uncertainly. "I have about $10,000 I had saved to spend in England when I got there. But instead I got this job with you. And I have some money in Australia. And there is my flat, but I have a mortgage on that and don't want to sell it. Why do you want to know?"

"I'd like to sell you the digital rights to all my books for $10,000," he said. "It's a good deal for you, and the notary is drawing up the contract."

33

"But . . . ," I stammered as Edward left the room.

The two books of Edward's that we had published digitally had been selling well and we were about to release the third one. They were making him a couple of thousand dollars a month and if the other books did half as well, then $10,000 for the digital rights was almost giving them away. He could live well for several years in the region of Spain we were in on what he had left from the English house sale, but as far as I knew, he had very little income coming in apart from dwindling print royalties. I had no idea if he made anything from the vineyards and winemaking.

I went in search of him and found him in the library looking at the manuscript for his unfinished novel. "I must finish this, Alex."

"Edward, what is going on? Why do you want to sell the digital rights? They are just starting to make you some money. And why would you want to sell them for so little?"

He looked away from me, and I knew he would prefer not to answer, but this was not something I could let him get way with avoiding. "I have to have some sort of an explanation, Edward."

He turned toward me, obviously not pleased at being pushed for an explanation. "Spanish inheritance laws are very strict, Alex. I am getting old, and if anything happens to me, I would like to ensure there is something for you. It was only because of you and your hard work that I even have these books still, and it seems a fitting way to repay your . . . services. You have been a very good secretary, and more." He picked up his pen and leaned over to start writing, but he stopped and smiled at me. "And, Alex, they are my books, and what I choose to do with the rights is my choice alone," he added.

I felt confused, grateful, and warmed that he would feel that way about me, but I also was concerned that he was giving up income he needed. And I wondered if he was tiring more easily now then he had a few months ago, if his health was not as good as I thought.

* * * *

The puppy, Cocky, was growing. I had to make her another bed as she had torn the first one to pieces and had chewed a big patch of paint off the central-heating radiator in a chewing frenzy as she lost her baby teeth. Keeping her supplied with things it was OK for her to chew became an effort. Monica assured me that the teething would be over in five or six weeks. I had also had to go into the notary several times to sign the papers assigning the digital rights to Edward's books to me, which had involved endless paperwork and the payment of various taxes. I longed for the next few weeks to be over and for my life to return to something more normal.

The second dog show date arrived in the middle of all that, and again Monica came and picked me and Cocky up. The show was supposed to go all day at an outdoor venue. Usually shows were held inside because of the changeability of the weather, but this one had been successfully run outside for some years. However, not this year.

When I got back home much earlier than planned I wondered if Edward's suggestion I get out more often was more for him than me. The show had been ended early by a sudden heavy storm and Monica dropped me off at the farmhouse as a youngish Spaniard came swaggering out of the front door, whistling. He threw a *Hola* our way, got into a small red sports car, and drove off. I wondered who he was and what he had wanted with Edward.

I took the puppy for a walk in the courtyard to relieve herself before I went upstairs to my bedroom to change. When I did I heard Edward's shower running as I walked down the hallway and wondered why he was taking a shower at that time of day. He never had before, he always showered at night, and I wondered again what the young man had been doing there. The images playing over in my mind got more erotic, and I was shocked to find how angry and jealous I

35

was at the possibility the young man and Edward may have been having sex while I was away. And the idea came to me that Edward may have gotten me the puppy because he wanted to get me out of the house to enable him to see someone else without me knowing.

Our relationship was undefined. We slept in separate rooms apart from a few hours once or twice a week. Edward was a restless sleeper and up several times in the night, and he had never encouraged me to stay the night in his bed, though at times I had. Edward did not introduce me as his partner. I was still recognized as his secretary, and we didn't go to social events together very often. When we did I was not there "with him," so to speak.

My jealousy surprised me. I had not even thought of being in love with him. I admired him, yes, respected him, yes, cared for him, yes. Was aroused by—yes, I was aroused by him. He was a competent lover, and in the dim light of his bedroom, his firm, lean body and experienced and satisfying lovemaking could have been that of a much younger man. I had not looked elsewhere for satisfaction since I had begun working with him. Perhaps that was love. Or because I was not highly sexed. I had no idea what he felt for me. But I immediately admitted I was wrong on that. I knew he cared for me. He showed it in many small ways. He had showed it by passing on the book rights to me for a nominal price.

What would I do, I wondered, if he stopped wanting me physically? If a younger, harder body attracted him more than mine. I had no idea. I tried to forget the incident. But of course I couldn't.

The next time Monica took me and Cocky to a dog show I couldn't help wondering what was going on back at the farmhouse. I hurried the packing up and lied about having an appointment in the late afternoon so she would drop me off earlier. When I got back Edward was in his study, working on his now almost-complete novel. There was no sign of any visitor having been there while I was out. I

36

confess that I even snuck into his bathroom to check if the shower had been recently used.

* * * *

The stone that covered his place in the mausoleum would not read Edward Michaels. His Spanish connections had been stronger than I could have imagined when we had moved to Spain, and this latest discovery—that he would have a place in a large family mausoleum in the grounds of the sixteenth-century church at O Carbello under another name, Edouardo Marce Pineiro, his Spanish birth name—was just the latest in the long list of Spanish surprises.

The extended family that arranged the funeral and did what was expected for a partner of a deceased was not completely a surprise as many had been there to greet Edward that first day we had arrived from England. But they were naturally uncomfortable with me, and there were signs of bitterness at how much Edward had passed on to me before he died. They had expected to benefit more from his death. Ivan's glances my way were ones that could kill.

He was the young man I had seen coming out of the house that day, whistling. I was greatly relieved when Ivan had appeared again on several occasions, attempting to make friends with the great-uncle he expected to inherit a great deal from. He failed. There was too much history between his grandfather and Edward. I hoped he didn't decide to do anything foolish. Spanish inheritance laws are complex, but he was never going to be able to claim he should inherit from me the farmhouse and vineyards that Edward had sold me the year before he died, guarded by the fact that we had married near the end. And Ivan had done well, getting the largest share of everything else, including Edward's old Rolls Royce.

I busied myself with the vineyard and gaining some American interest in the wines Pepe made. And I remembered the film we had been watching that had led to our first sex together. Although I missed him deeply, after a few months I knew that Edward was right: Life is too good to miss any of it. He had left a hole inside me, but maybe because we had not been a couple in the full sense for many years, it was not a bottomless hole. At thirty-seven I still felt young, and, thanks to Edward, I was comfortably off.

Edward had warned me early on against getting involved with Pepe or his son. He knew I found them both attractive. There were good reasons not to, he explained, and I had learned that myself, but understood why when he told me more.

I took to restoring the farmhouse and expanding the vineyards as a way to get over his loss and keep myself busy. I was also interested in adding tourist accommodation on the farm and starting vineyard tours of the area. With its picturesque riverside vineyards and centuries of wine production, the Ribeira Sacre, or Sacred River Bank, region was fast becoming a wine mecca for wealthy Americans.

# Chapter Three: Paul

"Let me get this straight. You're bisexual."

"Not too much," Xavier answered. We were sitting outside a coffee shop in the village of Guntin, where I had tracked him down. I was very much in shock and had to toss off a glass of brandy before my hands had stopped shaking enough to lift the coffee cup and hold it steady so as not to spill it all. He had the audacity to be sitting there, smiling at me, looking oh so sexy, and leaving his shirt open so that I'd remember how hard bodied he was.

"What do you mean 'not too much'? I don't think you can fuck both women and men and be just a little bit bisexual. And we both know you fuck men. Are you saying you don't fuck women? Or wasn't that your wife and your children you introduced me to at your house?"

He gave me a pained look, and it suddenly struck me that it was because I had used bald language. I laughed, but even Xavier could tell, I'm sure, that the laugh was bitter. He hadn't had any trouble with bald language when we were in the States. So, here, in Galicia, he suddenly had turned prudish?

"I like women mostly," he was saying. "Well, almost entirely. Yes, that was my family. I thank you for not saying anything they would not like to hear. But you did not tell me you would visit Spain—that you would visit me."

"Visit Spain? I've fuckin' moved to Spain—to be with you." Now that I knew that the language pained him, I used the words as bullets. I wasn't normally prone to obscene language myself. But I needed some sort of ammunition, some form of release—something to break through to him on how serious this was—how crushed I was.

"You did not tell me you had any such interest or intention," he repeated. I could tell that he was trying to be patient with me even though he thought I was being idiotic and presumptive. I didn't think that at the time, but after I'd left, gone back to the guesthouse in Lugo, and calmed down, I could clearly see his point. I was being both idiotic and presumptive—blinded by what I'd taken as deep mutual attraction. I hadn't told him I was going to visit him unannounced, much less move here.

"You like women mostly but you'll fuck men?"

"When I'm offered enough money to do so, yes. There are English expatriates here who are willing to pay quite a lot for sex. They like Spanish men. It's not an easy life here. Music takes much of the time I should be spending on the farm and it does not pay well. I can put a new roof on my house for what I made having the sex with you. If you would like to pay me to have sex with you, we can make arrangements, as long as you promise not to say anything to my family or come close to my farm again. You were good in bed."

"Paid? You were paid to have sex with me in the States? I didn't pay you."

"That Mr. Peters paid me."

"Ralph? Ralph Peters?"

"Yes, him. He told me to make you happy sexually. To make you want me and to think mostly about sex with me as we traveled around the States. I did make you happy sexually didn't I?"

"That bastard." It suddenly was clear to me. I'd been such a yutz. Ralph hadn't been too busy to squire Xavier around the States on his musical tour. Ralph had wanted to get me out of Washington so he could pitch his current live-in out and put the rush on Sean. If the fucker had just asked me to stand aside and let him pitch Sean, that would have been fine with me. He didn't have to get me all revved up to move to Spain to have a fairytale life with Xavier. And he damn well didn't need to make me look the cuckold in front of all of our mutual friends.

But then, Ralph hadn't made me make and carry through with those grandiose and impromptu plans any more than Xavier had. That all was on me. I'd been impetuous, which wasn't like me. But being impetuous had given me a thrill. I'd felt more alive in the last couple of weeks than I had for decades.

I should not have been blind to the insanity of this, though. Xavier's reservations on any form of romance—kissing or touching intimately. They hadn't just been his form of seduction, as unintentionally seductive as they had proved. He wasn't really into that. He was being paid for raw sex, and he'd set and maintained limits on what he'd do, what commitment he would make.

It was all on me in misunderstanding both what Ralph had been up to and what Xavier was willing to do. And to think I'd almost flown off the handle when I'd walked out to his small farm on the outskirts of Guntin after a frustrating nearly half hour trying to get directions in this town. I was learning all sorts of things about rural Spain in the four days I'd been here. I'd been so naïve about it all. Who would have known that not everyone in Europe spoke fluent English? And I hadn't even tried to find the house I'd bought yet. I was still struggling to drive my rental car on the narrow tracks they called roads here, and the real estate agent had wisely suggested that I master that before driving to my house.

Another unpleasant thing I had learned about this area of Spain was that it was on a latitude well north of Washington, D.C. More like Boston. I had thought "Mediterranean" and that I was escaping the cold of a late arriving spring. But I wasn't escaping anything—not even the weather. The weather was rawer here than what I'd left to

41

come here, and the heating of the houses—although the guesthouse was a modern building—was primitive in relationship to what I'd had in the States. The day I went in search of Xavier had dawned warm, though, which I took as a good omen in seeking Xavier out—a false good omen, as it turned out.

I'd almost blown it all as I approached Xavier's farm. He was out in front of the old stone house, which seemed to have all of the farm's outbuildings attached in one long, running wall, and was chopping wood. He was shirtless and looking extraordinarily desirable. I started to move toward him at a fast pace before he saw me, as concentrated as he was in wielding the axe. Luckily, I stopped in my tracks rather than call out to him and run to embrace him when I saw the first child—and then the second and third—come out of the door of the house. They were followed by a beautiful, dark-haired woman, who was drying her hands on the apron she was wearing. She said something to Xavier and touched him on the arm, and then he looked up at me.

The touch of her hand on his arm and the shock in his face when he saw me told me all I needed to know about what was what, who was who, and how I should act from that point, unless I wanted to be an ass. I don't know what he told his wife, but she beamed at me, curtsied a bit, and voiced what obviously was a welcome. She turned to the side and gestured toward the door. I knew she was inviting me to enter. I knew I couldn't do that. I knew I couldn't hold myself together much longer.

Xavier had recovered more quickly than I did. He said something to her and then suggested to me that we go back into the village, to a coffee shop, to converse. That seemed OK with his wife and it certainly was OK with me. I hope that I didn't give myself away to his wife and children. They all continued to smile, though, and I thought the smiles were genuine.

I felt like a worm. But at that point I thought that Xavier was lower than a worm. It was only later, at the coffee shop, that I placed myself lower than he was—and later than that, when I got back to the guesthouse in Lugo, that I realized I was the dumbest clunk on the planet. Still, I wasn't the world's lowest worm. That prize went to Ralph.

"You say you are moving here," Xavier said as he signaled for refills on our coffees.

"Yes, yes. I've bought a partially restored villa in the village of Friol," I said, feeling sluggish, knowing I was having a hard time focusing, accepting, catching up with reality.

"That's not far from here, if you have a car," he said. "I did enjoy the fucking with you. If you can pay, we can continue—"

"No, no, I don't think so," I said, abruptly standing up from the table, waving off the waiter who was approaching, and digging in my pocket for what I wanted to be more than enough euros to pay for the brandy and coffee—enough to make all of this just go away.

So, OK, maybe Xavier *was* a worm. I'd come to him in good faith and openly as gay and seeking. He'd been the one prostituting himself at the behest of a third party. And with a beautiful wife and three—or was it four—lovely children back in Spain. Maybe I was cutting him too much slack.

I just repeated the "No, I don't think so," a bit more forcefully and turned my back to him, not wanting to see whatever his reaction was, and marched back to the car I'd parked at the other end of the village.

* * * *

I was shaking like a leaf when I drove away from Guntin, and I had to pull over where there was hard earth on the verge of the road and rock back and forth behind the steering wheel, crossing my arms against my chest, and trying to regain my composure.

The shock not only of finding out Xavier's circumstances but also in discovering the key to his misleading behavior for the two weeks I'd escorted him around the States and had drunk deep of his mystery and charm had abruptly wakened me. I'd been asleep—in a dream—a wet dream. And while in that dream, I had made and carried out no end of stupid and precipitous decisions. I had closed out one life and signed up for another with a minimum of information and a maximum of gullibility. I hadn't put my apartment in the Watergate up for sale, thank God. It was premium property and would be snarfed up the moment I put it on the market, I knew. But I had bought a house in Galicia off the Internet, sight unseen. The blurbs on the house unabashedly admitted that it needed more renovation than it had received. What I'd seen of rural houses in the region since I got here told me that what had been admitted probably meant it was a crumbled ruin—or couldn't really be reached by anything justifiably claiming it was a road. Or both of those.

I wasn't meeting the real estate agent until the day after the next. I wasn't viewing what I'd already bought until then. I had pinned everything on Xavier being here to receive me—to have me and guide me through getting settled. I even had had visions of letting him redesign the house I bought to his likes. And now this. The dream was over. The nightmare was set to begin.

An older peasant was lurching by on an ancient tractor in the field next to where I had pulled the car off the road. Seeing me in the car in what I know must obviously have been a state of distress, he came off the tractor, trudged over to my rental car, and tapped on the passenger window.

I smiled wanly at him through a veil of tears I had managed not to release, shrugged, and started up the car to let him know I wasn't having car trouble. With another "nothing's wrong" wave and smile to him, I slow rolled back onto the road and pointed the car's nose toward Lugo and the guesthouse I was staying in—and whatever future in

Spain I had stupidly buried myself in at least until I could extract myself from the muck of what I, myself, had created.

The farmer had been gnarled and bent over—weather-beaten and ugly as sin. One thing I had been told before coming to Galicia was that life was hard on its men. By this reckoning, the farmer probably wouldn't have been any older than I was. But this hadn't been what I found when I got here. What I had marked in walking around in Lugo and had been informed of by the guesthouse host, Rafeal, was that most young Galicia men were handsome and muscular—this I had already noted—and that they tended to stay that way and virile into old age. It disheartened me to think that I'd be aging quicker than those around me.

It also scared me a bit that, as old and gnarled as the farmer was, what I was thinking as he walked up to the car was how well-endowed he was, fantasizing briefly of him entering the car and me straddling his lap and fucking myself on a juicy, timelessly hard Spanish cock. Somehow in this phase of insecurity and fearing for the flight of my sexuality and attraction to men, I was letting my mind run away with itself. That's what Xavier had done to me—what I was allowing a failed relationship with him to do to me.

I cursed myself—and Xavier as well—as I drove down the road. I couldn't help myself—it was, of course, mostly my fault and my stupidity, but I couldn't let Xavier off the hook either. I let myself entertain the nasty hope that when Xavier reached my age, he'd have rotted from the inside and be as old, ugly, and bent over as that farmer who had been willing to come to my aid on the road from Guntin to Lugo—the road back to reality, I had to hope. I couldn't help it; I hoped that when Xavier reached my age, he couldn't get it up for either man or woman.

\* \* \* \*

To say I was on edge when I returned to the guesthouse in Lugo, a private house really that had billed itself as the Catalunga Inn but that only had two rooms for rent—a double and a single—would have been an understatement. I was the only guest, booked in the single room, which was quite adequate and had a private bath. I had booked it off the Internet because it was listed as a gay-friendly property.

That it certainly was. The proprietor was a very good-looking Spaniard of about twenty-eight, who was friendly to the max and who wasn't shy about giving me the eye. He quite clearly was a bottom. He probably ran his house as a guesthouse for his personal pleasure. The house was something I would have expected to see in Northern Europe more than here—which may be one reason why I had been attracted to it on the Internet. It was a two-story, modern house, with stucco walls and wide expanses of glass looking out onto a terrace at the back where there was a swimming pool that ran the full length of the house. The Mediterranean touch was the ubiquitous red tile roof.

Beyond the host, there were a cook and a maid, but the host, Rafael, had made quite clear to me that the maid was only there for a few set hours in the early afternoon and that the cook kept to the kitchen area, which had windows opening on to an enclosed kitchen garden at the side of the house only.

He told me, with a wink, that the heated swimming pool couldn't be seen either from the servants' part of the house or any of the neighboring houses, "which makes it good for developing an all-over tan," he said, in case I couldn't get the inference already made. "It was designed for nude sunbathing and I take the sun out there frequently myself."

Also in residence was a set of beautiful Labrador Retrievers—a yellow lab bitch and a chocolate sire. The bitch had recently whelped, and when I returned from Guntin, Rafael and the dogs, the puppies in a large cardboard box, were in the back by the pool. The day being unseasonably warm, Rafael had been swimming. He was wearing a skimpy

46

Speedo that showed his body to be that of a willowy, well-proportioned twink when I first spied him at the pool. By the time I got out there, the Speedo had been shucked and he was half hard. He acted like there was nothing untoward in him being nude, however.

If I hadn't come back from Xavier's farm frustrated and in shock, I probably wouldn't have fucked Rafael. I would have had my emotions in control enough not to rush into a casual relationship. But Rafael obviously wanted me to fuck him. So I did.

It started with the dogs. I came out onto the terrace to let him know I was there. I tried my best to hide my distress from him by concentrating on the dogs. They were hard to ignore. I hadn't told Rafael where I was going and why, so I didn't have to field any questions on why I was back much sooner than I'd planned—and in shock.

He did ask why I seemed so wrung out and I mumbled something about the condition of the roads and how narrow they were. He let it go at that. He was obsessed with the dogs, which were beautiful animals, to be sure, so I figured that if I focused my attention on them too he wouldn't ask more probing questions about me being off kilter.

What my attention to the dogs, which included picking each of the puppies up and praising and playing with them, apparently did was to add to the interest Rafael already had in me. I think he saw me as a sensitive, kindred spirit and a dog lover when, actually, I had never had much to do with dogs to this point and could take them or leave them. In my weakened resolve state, I wound up taking both Rafael and one of the puppies.

Each puppy I picked up was an opportunity for him, crouched beside me by the box, to handle the puppy as well, showing me how to hold it, and according the opportunity for our hands to meet. And it provided the opportunity for our eyes to meet in shared smiles and expressions of delight in the puppies. And eventually for our lips to meet, for the last of the puppies to be deposited back into the box, and for me to bend Rafael over a pool bed, to go on my knees behind him, and to move my tongue into his crack and my hand around his dick. He, in turn, then sat on the pool bed, unzipped and freed me, and went down on my cock until it was engorged and throbbing. Again, there was no indication that we were doing anything illicit. He took the sex as natural, casual, and expected exercise. After he'd sucked me hard, I turned him onto his belly again, covered his body with mine, and mined his anal passage deep with my throbbing cock.

He took me with a yelp and heavy breathing subsiding into sighs and words of encouragement as he picked up the rhythm of the fuck in moving his channel back onto the cock. At length, I just held steady and he fucked himself on the shaft. It was clear we weren't doing anything that he didn't want to do.

The puppies squirmed in their box over each other's bodies, while the bitch and sire sat in interested attention beside the pool bed and watched me do to their master what the chocolate sire had done to the yellow bitch. I even used a position that would be familiar to them.

The first thing Rafael said after I'd shot my load and rolled off of him and into a sitting position between the puppy box and the pool was, "I'll move you from the single to the double, no extra charge starting tonight. We'll be more comfortable on the bed in there."

As nice as he was, from that moment I started to feel the bindings of possessiveness tightening around me. That didn't stop me from fucking him hard multiple times in multiple positions on that and subsequent nights in the bed I was renting, or to cause him to lose interest in my doing so.

By a week later, when I found that the stone villa I'd bought wasn't nearly as habitable as the Internet blurb had led me to believe, I moved to the Biterra Casa Rural countryside hotel northwest of my house in Friol, using the excuse that I needed to be closer to my house to keep a close eye on the renovation of that.

I left with a remembrance of Rafael and his open and eager hospitality—and legs. I named the chocolate lab puppy bitch I took with me Mandy after the first girl I had fucked on senior prom night before I had any inkling that I preferred men. Mandy, the girl, was as sweet and slobbery as Mandy, the puppy, was. At the time I left the Catalunga Inn I had no idea why I was leaving with a dog I had never intended to have. As time went on, though, I became a fanatical devotee to the concept that a man's dog was his best friend.

*  *  *  *

In later months when I ruminated on what was the nadir of my early days in Spain—at what point I was so low that I was one busy signal away from making plane reservations to fly back to the States for good—I surprised myself that it wasn't the day I stood in front of Xavier's farmhouse and watched his children and wife, one by one, come out of the door of their cottage. I had, even given the change and challenge it entailed, put all of my hopes and dreams into a life in Spain with Xavier. I hadn't even asked him if he cooked or washed clothes—I certainly didn't. And, obviously, I didn't ask him if he felt the same way about our short-lived relationship as I thought I did.

It wasn't even, surprisingly, when I was sitting in my car after that, watching an old, gnarled farmer walking toward me, and wondering if he had a cock I'd want to ride.

No, rock bottom in the early days of my Spanish adventure was the day the real estate agent drove me to Friol for the first time to see the house I had bought based on a description and photos on the Internet. I had thought I had worst cased what I would find. I hadn't. Thank God, though, that my real estate agent was a woman and had already figured out I was gay from my request for citations of gay-friendly hotels to stay at while the renovations had been completed on the house I'd bought. The house I'd paid cash for; the cash that the previous owners of the house had probably converted into the currency of some remote island paradise and had absconded to the night of closing and not left a forwarding address. I would have been embarrassed beyond recovery for a male real estate agent to see me crying.

In approaching the house I remember thinking that all of the stone farmhouses we were passing were quaint and might make good vacation houses if they underwent major renovations. I also made a note to buy a car with higher ground clearance and a narrower wheel base than the rental car I had or I'd never be able to get to my house. Muriel, the real estate agent, sensibly drove a smaller Land Rover—and I now know why she suggested that she drive me rather than letting me drive myself there. I didn't know if I wanted to sink that much money into a car, but I knew I would have to add another consideration when I was looking at a car to buy.

It wasn't so bad when we approached the house. It was a solid-looking, square, stone, two-story villa, with a stately demeanor and a small balcony over the entrance door. It was a solid, patrician look I had fallen in love with from the Internet. The windows looked new—wood cased, not vinyl—and the red-tile roof looked new too. This had been specified in the Internet blurb on the house. So did refurbished floors and staircase and bathroom. And it was true that the electricity and water were connected.

Beyond that, the blurb had been quite carefully, cleverly, and misleadingly written. The interior of the house was, in fact, not much more than a shell. The blurb had said nothing about interior walls. They were just the inner surface of the outer walls and lines of studs showing where interior walls had once been. There was no insulation, and that the electric and water lines were in was obvious, because they were exposed and running haphazardly around the walls. And what was there of the floorboards had been polished—

so technically refurbished—but there were gaps in the boards of the second-story floors and some of the planks bowed dangerously. The worst part about the gaps were that they told me immediately, upon looking down through the gaps in the floor, that I needed to get a sump pump going in the basement level.

I had assumed—falsely—that the mention of the renovated bathroom had been a typo in leaving off a plural "s," as the blurb clearly said there were two-and-a-half baths, which was quite impressive compared to the other properties I viewed on the Internet, but it was only the one bath that had been renovated. One of the others was just roughed in, which was actually less distressing than the main bath, where everything there had to be torn out and carted off while wearing protective gear. And, for my needs, the bath that was renovated was going to have to be gutted and completely redone before I would live there. It obviously would have to be—and marginally could be—tolerated in the interim.

Yes, the rooms were of pleasing proportions and there were four bedrooms upstairs, but there was no way I was going to be living here for some time. The house was about 2,400 square feet. It had cost me 130,000 euros, about $140,000, and by American standards the place was reasonably priced—it stood on nearly half an acre, albeit half an acre of wild undergrowth. But I could tell by the worried looks Muriel, the Realtor, gave me as we walked around the house, avoiding piles of debris and questionable-looking floor planks, that, by Spanish standards, I had been taken for a ride.

Silently, I went out onto the front steps, which too would need to be rebuilt to avoid lawsuits from any and all visitors, and sat hunched over, with face in hand. Muriel came out and produced a flask of brandy. She'd obviously come prepared for what I'd find and the effect it had on me. I now knew why she said nothing about moving directly into the house but, rather, had given me the names of appropriate—gay-friendly—inns and hotels in the Lugo and Friol areas.

I'd been a blind fool—blinded by the romance of the fairytale life I had woven that I would have with Xavier. I had figured that what little would need to be done could be brokered by Xavier at reasonable prices, because he was a local.

"I know of a couple of contractors who are reasonably good," she said gently.

Of course she did. It wasn't her fault, though. She hadn't foisted the house off on me and more than once had suggested that I take a look at it before making any commitments.

"The important thing is that the roof is new and water won't get into the house—well, the upper levels. That's when houses here really deteriorate—when rainwater gets inside. The contractors are brothers. They also are young and good-looking—and they both like men."

Of course they are good looking, and of course they are gay and randy, I thought. She was a great real estate agent. She thought of everything. I wondered if she knew the difference between a top and a bottom, though, and had been savvy enough to track down contractors for me who were bottoms. Well, I wasn't going to knock her. Having a flask of brandy to produce at this point indeed marked her as a great real estate agent. And I had no one to blame for this other than myself.

When I got back to the Catalunga Inn later that afternoon, the first thing I did was to take out the mobile phone I'd purchase for Spain and dial up the travel agency I'd used to get over here. As I listened to the busy signal, Rafael walked into my bedroom, nude, and knelt in front of me, unzipped my trousers, fished out my cock, and made me put the phone aside and forget it.

An hour later, I was about to dial again. Rafael had left the room but came back with Mandy for me to play with as she rolled around on top of the sheets that had been tussled by my calisthenics with Rafael.

"Are you trying to make the call again that you were making when I entered the room?" he asked. "You haven't told me how you had found your new house, but you didn't look pleased when you returned."

"There's nothing new about the house, Rafael," I said, as I rolled Mandy onto her back and rubbed her tummy. The fact that she held still for me, with her tongue lolling out of her mouth and her eyes full of worship, told me that she liked the tummy rub and that she liked me. I very much needed someone or something to like me at that moment. "What I'm doing," I continued, "Is calling the travel agency to book myself out of here and back to the States."

"Oh," he said, leaning over me and snatching Mandy up and holding her in his arms. "In that case, you won't want to be bonding with this puppy. It wouldn't be fair to her."

"I don't understand," I said. "I can take her to the States with me." The thought that I would came as a shock to me. I wasn't thinking this out any better than I'd thought anything else out for the last two months. But of course I'd take Mandy with me. We'd already bonded. I'd had no idea I wanted a dog until I had one. Of course I had no idea what the stipulations were about having a dog at the Watergate— but surely I'd seen others with dogs there. Of course the Watergate apartments were in the center of a city. I'd have to learn how to take care of a dog there. But, of course I would; other people had dogs in the city—although most of them weren't as large as Mandy was going to grow to be. "I don't understand," I repeated.

"She's just a puppy," he said. "She can't finish with her vaccinations for another three months. She can't leave the country until she does. And then there's a grueling airplane ride across the Atlantic. She's too young and delicate to withstand that. There's quarantine—thirty days, I think— on the other side. And she'd have to have a passport. She can't get that without proof of vaccination, and who knows how long it would take after that for a document to come through. No, the puppy's too young for all that. It wouldn't be fair to her. You'll just have to get another dog when you reach the States."

I didn't want another dog. I wanted Mandy. "A dog needs a passport to enter the States?" I asked, incredulous.

"Yes, of course."

And thus it was decided that I wasn't going to retreat to the States, defeated and with my tail between my legs. But only because I'd already bonded with a sweet chocolate lab that, four days earlier, I hadn't even known existed.

When I did make a phone call, it was to the Biterra Casa Rural hotel near Friol, which was nearer my house and where I could get a cheaper rate than here at Rafael's house—and, hopefully, a bit more privacy. I called to ensure that they would accommodate Mandy. She suddenly had moved way up there in my priorities.

\* \* \* \*

I was awakened by Anton moving from underneath my thigh and arm, rolling off the side of the mattress, rising to his feet, and sauntering off to the bathroom. I'd gone to sleep on my side, an arm embracing his chest; my thigh on top of his, pulling his body in close to mine; and my dick going flaccid in his ass. He didn't bother to close the door to the bathroom, and I could see him standing at the toilet, holding his cock in his hand, and pissing a long, beer-yellow stream into the bowl. He was good looking in the way that all men under thirty in this region seemed to be good looking. He was trim and well muscled from honest labor, tanned, dark and sultry, and slightly hirsute. His equipment was nothing to sneeze at, and he moved like a dancer and with pride, even in the nude. There was no self-consciousness in him for being naked, nor was there any reason for there to be any.

I needed to piss too now that I was awake and by the power of suggestion watching him do so, but I was as much pinned to the mattress on the floor of the villa's largest bedroom, otherwise devoid of furniture, as Anton had been. Uxio, the near twin of Anton in looks, was plastered to my back, his arm embracing my chest, his thigh over mine, and his dick, flaccid but long and very much buried, in my ass.

Muriel, my real estate agent, had said the two contractors she had in mind to do the renovation work on my villa in Friol were gay—and they had been proving that on a daily basis ever since they had shown up for work. In fact, they'd spent more time on this mattress—which they had brought—with me than they had in working on the house. And it seemed the more they worked, the more that was found that still needed to be done. It was a case of "aheader they went, the behinder they got."

Since the three of us were having a go mostly together, with various combinations of positions—including having worked up to double penetration—I was happy to learn that the two weren't brothers, as Muriel had thought. She probably was misled by them both having the same surname—Peres. But that was a common name in the region. They were cousins at some distance—I figured everyone in Galicia was—but far enough distant that they didn't mind fucking each other or me fucking them both at the same time, or both of them sharing my ass with their dicks.

I had done threesomes before, but rarely, and certainly not like this—or this often. I was paying them by the hour, regardless of what they were doing at the villa. At the rate that they were making progress on the villa, though, it would be over two years before I could move into the house, which meant not only paying them—essentially more for sex than for construction—but also paying my hotel bill. I rarely brought Mandy with me, and I was afraid that the staff at the Biterra Casa Rural would become so attached to her that they wouldn't let me bring her home.

Home. I still couldn't really think of the villa at Friol as home. It was still too rudimentary. It was turning quite warm, and the three of us worked in just shorts and construction boots. The Peres men were so gorgeous in the near altogether—and in the altogether—and I was so weak for man flesh, that whenever they were ready to go, so was I. And it seemed that any time we reached a point of getting into a major project, they wanted to fuck. I was beginning to believe that I knew as much about construction as they did.

I really did have to piss. Uxio was slowly awakening as I saw Anton's stream lessen and him wag the last drops out. I gingerly worked my way out from Uxio's embrace and moved to the side of the mattress. If he were fully awake, he wouldn't let me go without fucking me again. And he could manipulate me at will—not just because my will was weak but also because he was strong. He was, by far, the most muscular of the three of us. He also was the youngest, he had the biggest dick, he recovered and hardened the fastest, and, in most combinations, he was fucking me and I was fucking Anton.

Uxio was insatiable. It usually was Uxio who decided we needed a fuck break, and neither Anton nor I could say no to him.

I met Anton half way to the bathroom and we embraced and kissed before separating to take our divergent paths. He said something to me in Spanish and reached down and squeezed our cocks together, both of which started to harden up. My hardening was a little painful as I really had to piss. I couldn't understand his Spanish and he couldn't understand much of my English. That was part of the impediment to making progress on the renovations. What time we didn't spend fucking, we dedicated to just trying to have a meeting of the minds.

Once again I reminded myself that I needed to stop procrastinating on the Spanish lesson. But I was so bad at learning languages. I was much better at fucking. So, it wasn't surprising that I was doing more fucking than language study.

Speaking of which, Uxio was off the mattress and at my back, his big, calloused hands going to holding my hips, as Anton stroked our cocks together. Uxio's cock was at the small of my back, insistent.

"Just a few minutes, guys," I said. "I've got to take a leak first." But of course I said it in English, which meant nothing to them at all.

Anton came in with his lips for a kiss, While Uxio was lifting me off the floor and setting my ass, my channel still nice and open for him, on his cock. Anton grabbed the back of my thighs and hooked my knees on his hips, as his cock head too found my hole and pressed inside.

I still had to piss, but now I couldn't if I'd wanted too. The hardening factors had taken over and the rise of semen was taking over the priority role. I moaned as the two Pereses held me between them, with them standing and crouching a bit for stability, as they pistoned my channel together. All three of us came almost simultaneously. The piss factor took over again immediately, and I struggled out from between them and made a dash for the bathroom.

They were both laughing in the wake of my escape.

When I came out of the bathroom, they were dressed, downstairs, and in the front yard of the villa, gathering up their tools. The shadows were long. Their habit was to arrive late and leave early in the day and to break up their long lunch break with fuck sessions.

I went down the stairs—I enjoyed going up and down the stairs in the villa as the staircase was the only part of the house that had a finished and solid feel to it—and sat on the front steps and watched them pack up.

They were two beautiful young men, and I was addicted to their idea of a work day. But this just couldn't go on this way. Spring was moving on, and I needed to be able to live in the house before winter set in. The heating system hadn't even been planned out yet. There was no way I was going to live in this house with its thick stone walls without better heat than the people here seemed satisfied with. I'd freeze before fall was half fleeted.

I somehow had to get workmen here who would work faster and more efficiently. And I'd have to ratchet back on the side benefits of the Peres cousins.

# Chapter Four: Alex

I filled my time with work: the vineyards; renovating the manor house, or Pazo Carbello, as it was known locally; and managing the converting of the old buildings into tourist accommodation. I also had Cocky by me always and discovered the great company a dog can be, but she was no replacement for an intelligent and articulate companion who shared my interests. I needed intellectual company.

I went to bed tired each night, but I was lonely in bed too. After the funeral I had moved into Edward's room, because he had asked me to, gaining comfort from being in the bed we had shared.

Edward and I had certainly not had acrobatic or earth-shattering sex all over the house, but I had been well satisfied. He was an affectionate man in private. He was a wonderful kisser and uninhibited about it, and he loved to touch and be touched. There was no part of my body he had not kissed or run his hands over numerous times. Even my feet had pleased him. And there was no part of him I had not tasted or touched at some time. He had been concerned about looking old and had preferred to have sex in dim light. It was flattering to him. His cock was still working well, which pleased us both, but the sag of the skin on his flat stomach and thighs embarrassed him.

Often he would turn on the lamp at my side of the bed, throw back the covers, and make love to my body. "So young and firm," was his mantra at these times.

In the evenings when we relaxed together watching TV or a video or listening to music, we sat close on the sofa and either his head or mine rested on the other's shoulder. Our hands lay on each others' bodies and we'd kiss occasionally and perhaps put our hands to more erotic use as bedtime approached.

Even in the last months we had often lain together in his sickbed, feeling and enjoying each other, his cock still able to stiffen and ejaculate almost to the end—something that pleased him greatly.

Physically, I felt his loss deeply. But I was reluctant to look for comfort or affection from casual sex.

In my late twenties I thought I had found the one true love. Rus. He was a dentist and a strong and imaginative lover. We had fucked all over the house in creative positions. Mainly positions of his devising. I had enjoyed it. But I had also believed the desire for that sort of wild sex had shown how much he wanted me, loved me.

Then one evening he brought home a young guy, a good-looking stranger, and assumed I'd want to be in an athletic threesome. Maybe I would have agreed, but the guy he had brought back made the mistake of saying he'd go to the bathroom while Rus and I discussed it. He went straight there and I immediately knew he had been in our apartment before. Any arousal I had felt for the idea of a threesome with him had instantly died and, instead, I confronted Rus.

"He's been here before, hasn't he?" I said angrily, hoping he'd say something that would make it OK.

Rus shrugged and smiled that cheeky, sexy, sultry smile he had. "We aren't married Alex. I like variety and you must have other guys too sometimes."

"No I don't," I spat back. "I thought we were in love. We may not be married but . . ."

"Come on, Alex. Relax. He's great in the sack. You'll enjoy the change."

Change. There are times when you change your feelings about someone in a moment, and that was the

60

moment I stopped loving or even liking Rus. I left the flat and walked the streets for a couple of hours, but it solved nothing. Then I went back and made up the bed in the second bedroom, the one Rus had never actually moved into. I could hear him and his friend going at it in the next room. I admit there was something arousing about it. But I shut it out as best I could. I had no intention of joining them.

I have to say it put me right off sultry men who wanted to have wild uninhibited sex when they first met me. Not that many had.

\* \* \* \*

I admit that I often dreamed of Pepe or Jacobo, or both. I often spent time with them in the vineyards or the bodega and always felt aroused. But when we first arrived at the pazo Edward had asked me to promise that if I needed more than he could give me I'd go elsewhere, not to them.

I may have broken my promise not long after. During the first grape harvest I was in Spain for we had often brushed against each other, Pepe and Jacobo and I, and it was only knowing I had promised and also had Edward to fuck me when I got back to the house that stopped me succumbing. I was certainly tempted.

But before the next harvest I had started to keep my distance from them.

"If Uncle Francisco had stuck to fucking the old man instead of trying to change the world, we could own this vineyard now."

I heard Pepe say it. The way he said it was angry. My Spanish had improved a great deal, though I made silly mistakes and preferred not to talk the language much to Spaniards. I had just left the bodega after telling Pepe and Jacobo that Edward had asked me to manage the vineyard. I'd stopped outside the door to check something, and Pepe had spoken in anger, and probably louder than he realized.

I still knew little of Edward's life in Spain before he left for England. But I did now know that he had left because of the disappearance of a close friend of his who was actively anti Franco. Edward had shared his friend's sympathies as well as his body, and after Francisco's disappearance Edward's family had decided that going to his late mother's family in England for a few years would be best for everyone. His English mother had died when Edward was ten.

Edward had agreed to go, but not temporarily; he had turned his back on Spain. I now knew that this explained the thread of isolation and lack of belonging that ran through Edward's books. He had spent nearly forty years ignoring his Spanish roots, only relenting as his father was dying.

"Family is more important as you get older, Alex," he said to me when he told me about Francisco. "I only returned to Spain when my father was dying. He spoke to me on the phone and told me how much it mattered to him to see his oldest son once again." He paused. "Family is what we are, but it is our lovers who can make us more than we are. Francisco made me see the injustice in my country, and because of him I lived much of my life in England, which was kind to me. You have given me great happiness and rekindled my desire to write and my pleasure in life, Alex. I cannot imagine what it would be like to be back here without you. Without seeing all this, my home and my people, through your eyes. Without having such great affection here in this house, where I had some terrible times before I left."

I had been deeply moved. The longer I was there and the more Spanish I spoke and the more Spanish literature I read the more I came to see how its history, its rulers and wars, really were part of the present here. Not like Australia, a place with little past and little history. It had none of the events, terrible events usually, like civil wars and invasions, persecutions and repressions, that shape nations and their people.

After overhearing Pepe I understood why Edward had warned me not to get involved with him or his son. It would be too complicated. And I had no intention of perhaps being the avenue for Uncle Francisco's relatives to gain what they felt he had failed to get for them.

\* \* \* \*

It was Cocky who got me my first lover after Edward, but things couldn't have started in a worse way. It was late, about 10:00 p.m. I was in my office working and she was under my desk chewing on a bone when she started coughing and making horrible crying noises. The crying got louder as she came out from under the desk, pawing roughly at the right side of her mouth, leaning on me, and looking up into my eyes, begging me to help her.

I was in shock. She had never had any illness or injury before, and I had little experience with dogs. I tried looking in her mouth, but she was so distressed I feared I might lose a finger. I was in a panic and rushed for the phone. I could not get the usual vet, which made me more distraught. My hands shaking, I dug out a dog magazine in which I remembered seeing an ad for a new local vet. I had trouble dialing and almost collapsed in relief when he answered on the second ring.

He told me to bring Cocky straight in. I carried her to the car and sped dangerously fast. In ten minutes we arrived at his surgery and he was already unlocking the door. I carried her in though she was quite capable of walking. In spite of her distress she had seemed to calm a bit when she saw she was going in the car.

"So, she has something in the mouth?" he said in broken English.

"Si" I replied, "*Masticaba un hueso cuando de repente estaba en el dolor y muy afligida,*" I added, not sure why he was speaking English to me.

"Ah, so a bone has got stuck in her teeth," the vet said, with a concerned look. "You speak good Spanish. On the phone you were mixing Spanish and English."

"It must have been the panic," I replied, surprised.

"I can see the bone," he said, peering into her mouth while holding the jaw gently. He got a pair of forceps.

"Hold her steady, please," he directed.

I held her and talked soothingly in her ear and he maneuvered the forceps inside her mouth, occasionally brushing my arm with his as he did. His face was close to mine, so I could see each hair of his five-o'clock shadow. There was a small jerk and a sharp yelp and the forceps emerged with the piece of bone in them. Cocky closed her mouth for the first time since it got stuck and shook her head as if to clear the pain away. The curved-shaped bone was smaller than I had expected.

I relaxed and thanked the vet profusely, touching his shoulder. I was now also able to appreciate that the vet was a beautiful man. Lean and elegant, he reminded me of Edward. But he was also young, and his way with Cocky showed he was sensitive and caring. It was enough to start me humming and I felt myself going hard.

"I am sorry to get you out so late. I hope I didn't spoil your night," I said, mildly embarrassed at what I was feeling.

"No, I am glad you called. She needed to see me. And I was doing nothing but watching TV." He smiled an incredibly sexy smile.

"Can I buy you a drink?" I offered, surprising myself. "To thank you. The cafés are still open, aren't they?" I added uncertainly, as I had been out to cafés and restaurants very seldom since arriving in Spain.

"Of course they are," he replied. "This is Spain and a Friday night. A drink would be better than going back to the TV, and I know a café just nearby where Cocky can sit by the table."

Now that the excitement was over Cocky went to sleep as soon as we sat down at the café, which really was only a few doors from the clinic.

The vet's name was Jose. I told him mine.

"Ah so, you live at Pazo Carbello," he said.

"Yes."

Everyone knew who was who locally. "You must miss your partner," he added.

"Yes. It has been three months now but . . ."

He touched my hand. "I have coffee and wine at my house," he said. "I make good coffee and my father makes good wine that he gives me more than I need of."

It turned out his house was close to the surgery and not the bachelor's house I had expected. Inside it was cool and big and modern and he poured wine and led me to a small terrace.

Cocky had made herself at home and was almost instantly asleep on the mat in front of the sofa.

"She is completely over it," I said.

"Yes, dogs do not dwell on things like we do. They get on with enjoying being alive."

"It is important to enjoy being alive," he said, and he laid a hand on my thigh and leaned in for a kiss. I met his lips half way and lay a hand on his shoulder to steady myself. He moved his hand to my package and felt how hard I was.

"Mmm, nice," he murmured. He moved a hand to my chest and up under my T-shirt and squeezed my nipples and stroked my belly. I was breathing heavily and wanted him to fuck me.

"I think . . ." I mumbled, feeling I might come soon.

"You want me to make love to you?" he asked in a husky voice.

"Yes," was all I could say as our mouths met again and he was unzipping his pants and moving my hand to a hard and long cock. I stroked it, feeling it get even harder. So young, and so hard, I thought—Edward's favorite phrase of appreciation. Though Jose was not much younger than I was he was a lot younger than Edward had been.

Jose pulled me up and led me to a bedroom, where he pushed me to my knees to suck his cock. I pulled his jeans down to his ankles as I sucked, revealing his lean, muscular legs with a light coating of long, black hairs. I ran a hand up and down the silkiness of them. His cock emerged from a glossy bush and moved in and out of my mouth as he guided my head back and forth slowly. Then he got rougher as his juices rose, making me gag, before stopping and pulling back. I stood and we kissed again as he stripped off my clothes roughly and I stripped off his shirt. He kicked off his jeans, tossed me back on the bed, and crawled up over me. He made rough stabbing kisses at my mouth and face and neck, nipping me lightly sometimes before pulling back. Meanwhile, I ran my hands over his body, enjoying the feel of his silky body hair, he stroked my cock and his own knocked against my belly.

When I begged him to fuck me he moved down my body, nipping and licking until he was at my cock. He sucked it briefly before pushing my legs back and moving his knees under my hips. He rubbed lube into my hole and finger fucked it into me. I moaned and reached for his nipples, dark and circled by long, black hairs. He reached into the bedside table for a condom and had me roll it on him. He entered me hard. I arched my back up at the shock of his entry but cried out more with pleasure than pain as he went deep inside me.

He fucked strongly. Long, firm, deep strokes that had me arching my back again and again as I moved with him and drew him deeper. I quickly spouted my cream up his belly and mine. He came deep inside me, then pulled out, tossed the condom aside, and we began to kiss and fondle again, both of us going hard quickly. This time he doggy fucked me, his length making its mark even deeper inside me. When we came I collapsed on the bed, panting and with all the tension gone from me.

We lay in a loose embrace as we recovered, but it was broken by his mobile phone ringing. Jose hurried to answer it and left the bedroom to talk to the caller. I immediately thought it could be another emergency and got up guiltily, hurrying into my clothes and out of the bedroom. He was just saying good-bye and shutting the phone off when I got to the living room.

"I had better go," I said. "And Cocky needs to get back home."

He was standing there naked and beautiful.

"You don't have to go," he said. "It was not an emergency."

"I had better. But . . . but, would you like to meet again?"

"Of course. It was nice, and I like you," he said with a smile and moved in to kiss me. We kissed and hugged till we were both stiffening, when he broke the embrace with a smile. I staggered out of the door with Cocky following and floated home.

In bed I fantasized about Jose and I fucking again and stroked myself off to yet another ejaculation. In the morning it all seemed like a dream. I was wondering when to call him when he phoned me. We arranged to meet for lunch at his house the following day, as the surgery closed for the typical two hours in the middle of the day.

I decided Cocky would need company, because I hoped I might be away from home a lot in the future. I didn't see Jose being comfortable at the pazo. I decided I'd go in search of another puppy when I had time. Monica and I still went to dog shows together, but she had already recommended I get my next dog from another breeder, an internationally well-known kennel owner near Lugo.

I rang the bell and Jose opened the door naked and erect. I was instantly aroused by his body and the hint of danger of the neighbors seeing us. He pulled me in and stripped off my clothes as we moved, mouth glued to mouth and my hands roaming over him, toward the bedroom.

Again he pushed me back onto the bed, but this time he went straight for my hole and, after little preparation, entered me forcefully and fucked me hard and fast to his first ejaculation.

"I am sorry," he murmured, pouting. "I was so much anticipating you. The second time is for you."

He then finished me off slowly while we kissed and I stroked him back to hardness. He did as promised, sucking me till I was stiffening again then kissing over my body and nipping lightly at my nipples and belly as he did. He pulled the drawer open to get out another condom and I glanced in at the photo of a woman in there. It barely registered. I rolled the condom on his long cock and guided it to my hole, and he fucked me slowly before pulling out and turning me over and doing me doggy style, while he slow pumped my cock, bringing me nearly to coming then backing off. Finally, I was begging him to let me come. He did and then we fell together on the bed for a brief time with his cock still buried inside me.

When he pulled out he went straight to the bathroom and I rolled over to see the clock showing three forty and that the Spanish lunch break was nearly over. I opened the drawer to put the clock inside, not wanting to know that our time was nearly up, and again I saw the picture of the woman. But this time I saw the whole photo. Jose was on one side and she was on the other and their arms were about each other.

I still had the drawer open when he returned from the bathroom.

"You should not look in there," he said, with a smile. "There is no time for another fuck."

"Who is she?" I asked, pointing to the photo and hoping he would say something to make it all right.

He paused, then said it. "That is my wife. She has been in Argentina on family business for a long time. I am sorry if you did not know. Everyone here knows I am married."

"No, I didn't," was all I could say as I got off the bed and picked up my clothes and headed for the bathroom

"I am sorry you did not know. . . .if you thought . . ." Jose said as I left and I believed the look on his face was genuine.

I managed to exit the house without embarrassing myself.

* * * *

When I got home, I decided Cocky still needed company. There was no need for both of us to be lonely.

# Chapter Five: Paul

"Heel. Heel. Damn it to hell, bitch, get back here."

Mandy paid no attention to me whatsoever. She'd be laying down next to me, all contented, wanting to hang her muzzle on my foot, but if one of Homero's men walked by across the lawn, taking building supplies into the Friol house, up she'd jump and be lunging at them. It was her friendly bark and lunge. She just wanted to play. No reason for them to know that, though.

I had her on a chain that didn't reach the pathway the workmen were using, and she was just a puppy. A Labrador Retriever puppy was still a formidable object, however, even though she just wanted them to notice her and to play with her.

Well, I'd be happy if they noticed and played with me too—especially the young hunk, Noé, but that wasn't happening. I was lying out here in a broken-down bamboo lounge chair on my front lawn while Homero and his crew were working on the house. I was bare-chested, taking in the late summer Galician sun, barefooted, and in short shorts. Anton and Uxio would have noticed. They'd be swarming around me, being suggestive, and coaxing me to carry through on those suggestions, rather than working on the house. But not Homero's crew. Not Noé or Alberte, nor Homero himself who, though older than I was was still good-looking and hard bodied.

But then, if my original work crew, Anton and Uxio, had been here and flirting with me, coaxing me to come in and go to bed with them, they wouldn't be working on the house. And therein lay a big part of the reason I'd dismissed them—gently and with considerable cash in hand—and engaged a more expensive, but more expert and all-business contractor from Santiago to accelerate and finish up the restoration of the old villa I had bought in Friol. What had pushed me over the edge with sending off Anton and Uxio, to my shame, wasn't their interest in sex over work. Sex with them had grown to be my primary interest as well. It wasn't just that they were shagging me more than working, it was because I'd caught them skimming building materials to use on projects of their own.

This being an area where everyone was related to everyone else and knew their business, I couldn't call them on their theft without being shunned—indeed I had to consider by minor skimming was accepted here—so I just paid them off with a smile and said they were exhausting me sexually. That part was true, but we all really knew why I sent them off. Since it wasn't spoken, however, it never happened and everyone was just pleased as punch.

And the summer season wouldn't last forever. Inevitably, autumn would be approaching, which would be followed by winter. I needed insulation, running water, reliable electricity, and central heat before the cold set in.

Still, it wouldn't have hurt to take a short break now and again for a friendly fuck or two. Homero was older, but hard bodied. Alberte was not much younger than I was and a bit ugly, but hard bodied. And Noé was young, quite well turned out, and hard bodied. I was getting a hard on just thinking about any of them, but Mandy was distracting me from that.

"No, girl. Sit. Come back here." Alberte had passed again with two two-by-fours hefted on his shoulder, and Mandy had taken a run at him, only falling back on her haunches when the length of the chain wouldn't let her get there. She howled in frustration and gave him a series of "Hey, I'm over here" barks. I could almost hear her crying, "Play with me. Whatcha' doin' in the house? Why can't I go in there with you, huh, huh, huh?"

No discipline at all. Absolutely no sense that I was the master and she should listen to me. When Rafeal had sold her to me, he claimed that Labs were highly trainable. That I didn't have a hint how to train her to do my will wasn't taken into consideration. I guess I had expected Mandy to figure that out. She hadn't.

There she was, at the length of the chain, not coming back to me on command. Just sitting on her haunches and being "Who, me?" cute. Alberte was well past her now. Rather than come back to me, though, she went down on her belly on the ground and was gnawing on something, waiting, no doubt, for Alberte to come back out of the house.

With a sigh, I picked up the book I was trying to read—not being successful in getting far at each go, even though it was a well-written book I'd picked up because it was about this region—Domingo Villar's *Death on a Galician Shore*. The reason I wasn't getting absorbed in the read was the same reason Mandy wasn't coming back to me. She was panting for one of the workers to come back out of the house. I was panting for sexual attention. In some ways it had been a mistake to let Anton and Uxio go, because they took care of my basic need—a need that was high in my concern at the moment.

My cell phone rang. I had been just letting the phone ring, not taking any calls because I didn't have much cheery news to report on my move to Spain yet. Mandy was the cheeriest thing I had going for me at the moment. With a sigh, though, I opened the connection. It was my old law partner and sometime lover, Holland Howard, all the way from Washington, D.C.

"Hey there, good buddy. Ready to come to your senses and trot back to civilization?"

"Still leading the good life here, chum," I answered. As I did so, I looked over at the house. The second-floor windows, frames and all, had come out this week for full replacements. What had originally looked like new window frames had just been a clever staining job. It looked like a bomb had blown them out. The yard needed tended to; the grass, if you could call weeds that, had grown up so that it would be hard for me to find the manual mower that was out here somewhere. Mandy was noisily chewing on something and not heeding my commands. I'd run out of vodka—two days ago—and I didn't have a clue how one bought liquor around here—the handling estate agent, Muriel, had initially stocked me up. I hadn't laid anyone in a week and my balls ached. Yeah, life here was just hunky-dory.

"Well, I'm serious, Paul. We want you to come back to Washington. We all miss you, and I've discovered that I need your memory and expertise in the law office as well. You don't have to come back to the office, just take on consultancy for good pay status."

"Oh, 'we' all miss me? Our law partners who found out I'm gay but haven't found that out about you yet miss me? Sean misses me? Ralph misses me?" I wasn't anywhere close to forgetting that Ralph had set me up for a fall with a Spanish guitarist—which had led to my futile and impulsive mid-life-crisis move to northwest Spain in the first place. He'd set me up to be gone on a national tour with this Spanish hunk so that he could steal my live-in, Sean. Not that my relations with Sean by then precluded the desire that someone take him off my hands.

"Sean's gone. It didn't last more than two weeks— Sean being with Ralph. And Ralph is contrite. He says there's no one he can lean on when singing his part in the Gay Men's Choir. He wants you back as much as I do."

At that moment I could have cried. I'd spent the last month kicking myself for impulsively pulling up stakes and moving to Spain in pursuit of a man who was happily married here and who had been paid by someone to seduce me. And I'd just had to cash in some bonds to throw money at winterizing this house—this money pit—that I'd bought sight unseen and, after a month of renovation, still looked like a World War II bombing victim. And I couldn't even get my damned dog to heel. I was sorely tempted to go home. But I also was not one to snuffle back with my tail between my legs.

"It's a thought, Holland," I answered. "Something I can think about and laugh about with my young Spanish lover, as we gorge on Spanish gourmet fare and fine wine under candlelight in this palace I have here in Galicia before we go upstairs and fuck in the bathtub."

We both laughed. He told me again that he was serious, and I let him work me down to a "I certainly will think about it." I managed to click off before I sank to what I wanted to say: "Daddy, come rescue me, please."

As I disconnected from the conversation with Holland, I saw the younger hunk, Noé, coming out of the house and walking down the path to Homero's truck. Then I heard a crash and cursing in Spanish from one of the rooms on the front on the second floor. I'd told Homero I thought the ceiling in there was about to come down.

Then I realized what I hadn't heard. I hadn't heard Mandy barking or baying at either of these occurrences. I turned my eyes to where I'd last seen her. She wasn't there. I got up and walked quickly to the other end of the chain. What the bitch had been chewing on was the leather loop attaching the chain to her collar. It was chewed open, and she was gone.

After searching the yard, and being almost swallowed in bushes badly in need of trimming, without finding Mandy, I went into the house. She was sitting quietly and obtrusively in an upstairs bedroom doorway and watching the workman gathering up the bedroom ceiling into a wheelbarrow. She was smiling and contentedly lolling her tongue and lightly panting—panting like I panted when Xavier, the Spanish guitarist, turned the scene on me and fucked me. She didn't lose the smile when she saw me come up the stairs, the chain looped on my arm. Even though I wasn't smiling. Even though I called her to come to me. She just smiled at me and turned her head to go back to watching Homero and Alberte working in a cloud of plaster.

I left the upstairs landing, walked down the staircase, the only solid construction in the house yet, and out onto the lawn. Picking up the cell phone I'd dropped in the seat of the bamboo chaise, my finger hovered over the "last call" button. I could call Holland back, tell him I'd fly back to Washington as soon as I could arrange it—that this impulsive move to Spain had just been me not thinking straight. I could be done with a house that didn't want to be renovated and a dog that disdained me.

But this too would be impulsive, I realized, and I'd never been a quitter. Checking through the index of numbers in the phone, I hit the button of the only one here who I thought could help me with the most immediate of my problems, but one. My most immediate problem was that I badly was in the need of a lay. There was no one on my index close enough to help me with that. I had erased Anton's and Uxio's numbers in ire right after I'd fired them. In fact, the only number in Spain that was in my index yet was a woman.

"Hello, Muriel? Help!" Muriel was the estate agent who had negotiated the sale of this villa to me. I couldn't blame her for my buying the villa, though. I had done that to myself all by myself, buying it sight unseen over the Internet. Muriel was just the one who kept me from shooting myself the day she brought me here and who had saved me from shooting myself, with her good humor and help, all the succeeding times I had wanted to do that.

Without hesitation, she asked me what I needed. I would have thought she had a crush on me, except she had sent Anton and Uxio to me, knowing, at the time, that I needed sexual release more than I needed the villa renovated.

"It's this dog of mine, Mandy," I said. "I simply must get her to obey. Do you know anyone who does owner-dog obedience training?"

"Not off hand," she answered after a bit of pondering. "But I do know a vet who will know. Jose Reis. You could contact him. But he's a good bit south of here, in Chantada. That's a good fifty kilometers by road."

"I'm desperate, and I've been meaning to explore the area a bit. Can you arrange an introduction for me and help me set up an appointment?"

I knew that making contact through mutual acquaintances was "the way" to do business in Galicia. Muriel readily agreed, and in no time I had a typically Galician appointment to see this Jose in his vet surgery "sometime" two days hence.

I went into the house to see which of the workers I could bribe to keep track of Mandy for two days, starting the next evening. There was no way I was taking her with me. The cage I had for her was plastic. She'd be chewed out of that before I got as far as Lugo. And before I got to Chantada, the backseat of my new car would be in shreds.

I knew, though, that, although Mandy would be curious why I was missing, if I left her with one of these hunky Galician construction workers, she'd be in heaven.

\* \* \* \*

The drive down into the southern hilly, river valley of Galicia reminded me of how attractive I'd found this part of Spain when I'd first arrived. It certainly wasn't either the arid topography of central Spain or the resort-strip Mediterranean coastline of the Costa Del Sol that I'd expected to see. Every picturesque stone village house I passed—and they were there at every turn—I compared with my own stone villa, and the condition of mine withered in comparison to many of these. But then I was in a sour mood—or I was when I

76

started. The scenery on the drive down the N540 mellowed me with each passing kilometer.

That lasted until I got to Chantada, managed to find Dr. Reis' vet surgery, and found the door locked and a note pasted to it. My Spanish was close to nil, but a passing bicyclist was good enough to stop and tell me that the vet was closed for lunch. I'd been in Spain long enough to know that wasn't going to be a fifteen-minute break.

I decided to have lunch myself and went over to an outdoor café at the edge of a square that overlooked the small river running through the town, the Rio Asma. The food was good and the wine was better, this being the center of the Ribeira Sacra and Ribeiro wine regions along the Mino river and its tributaries south of Lugo. But best of all was the view of the young Spanish men walking the square. I was still very much in a horny mood. I really needed to get laid.

It took me a while to realize that there was a young man sitting alone at a table near me who had managed to tune into my need. Perhaps he had watched my eyes following the young men as I lingered over coffee after the meal. Or perhaps he'd seen my hand drop to my basket more than once while ogling the men—or the wide stance I took because of my aching balls or even the hardness of my basket.

I became aware that he was lingering at the café as long as I was and then I began exchanging glances and, eventually, smiles with him. He was a beautiful young man. Not more than twenty, with dark, sultry looks and jet-black curly hair. His body was slight, and he was clothed in a tight athletic T-shirt, with plunging arm holes showing the tufts of curly pit hair, a plunging neckline that showed the cleavage of a nicely muscled chest, shorts, and flip-flops. I was thinking thoughts of holding him suspended in front of me and pulling that small body of his on and off my cock several minutes before he stood and came over to my table.

"Excuse me. You don't seem to be expecting anyone else. Do you mind if I—?"

77

"Not at all," I said. "Please have a seat." I'd said that in English without giving it a thought. I probably could have managed it in Spanish if I wasn't enthralled with him and my balls weren't aching so for attention.

"Ah, you are English. Good. I'd hoped . . ."

"American, actually. You'd hoped to meet an Englishman?"

"No, no. An American is even better. I had hoped you spoke English—so that I can practice a bit my English."

"Your English is excellent. It probably is I who needs to practice my Spanish. But why is being an American better than being English?"

He laughed, gave me a shy "should I or should I not say it" smile, and, no doubt decided he could from the "desperate for sex" vibes I obviously was exuding. His face took on a coquettish aspect, and he answered, "Because American men are so much more generous than Englishmen." Then he named a price that he probably considered quite generous but that I considered a bargain.

It was my turn to laugh. "How did you know? Do I look that desperate?" It was a rhetorical question, really. I *was*, in fact, that desperate.

"You look like someone I very much want to be with," he answered. "Do you think our River Asma down there is very pretty? There are several very private and lovely isolated spots on the banks of the river close by here. Very private. I could show you."

In a small space between towering bushes at the side, a stand of trees at our back, and the Rio Asma in front of us, I leaned back into a tree, my legs spread and slightly bent, my trousers and briefs off, while the young Spaniard knelt between my legs and gave me an extra-fine "almost" blow job that could have been completed if he didn't let me spin it out to fucking him. Holding me off so that he could go down, fully stripped, on the small of his back between the roots of the tree, his back against the tree trunk, and his fingernails dug into my biceps, as, on my knees between his

78

thighs and his bent legs, held under my arms, I pulled his pelvis up to mine, entered him after rolling on a condom, and pumped him to a needed ejaculation.

It was relief I needed badly, and he left me there, snoozing and gazing into the racing water of the Asma, for a good half hour before, groaning in satisfaction, I pulled myself up, redressed, and headed back up into the town.

The door to the vet's surgery was still locked, but there was a different note on the door. The passerby I stopped to help me decipher the note, said the office was closed for the EuroBasket Championship semifinal and gave me a "have you had your head in a hole?" look when I showed I didn't know what the EuroBasket Championships were and why that meant a vet would close up early— especially when he knew he had someone coming to talk to him today.

I was planning to stay overnight anyway so I didn't grouse very long. I decided to take a ride around the area, check out some of the wineries, and look for somewhere to stay. Muriel had given me a list of guest houses in the region. By dusk, I was nearly sloshed from the wine drinking and running on empty on places to stay. Everything was booked, this being a high tourist season. Everyone was sympathetic and trying to be helpful, though. They made suggestions of places that hadn't been on Muriel's list—none of which panned out—and almost universally suggested that I probably could do better back in Chantada itself.

By the time I got back to Chantada, it was time to eat again, so I decided to tackle that at what looked like a local pub before looking for lodging. When I entered the pub, I saw that they were in the midst of a riotous celebration. I'd seen evidence of that on the streets of Chantada while I was parking—men running through the streets, yelling at the top of their lungs, and waving banners and the Spanish flag.

The TV sets were all on when I entered the pub, all turned to commentary following a basketball game. When I ordered something that essentially was the same as I knew as a shrimp po' boy sandwich and a beer, the bartender told me that Spain had just won the semifinal of the EuroBasket Championships.

That explained the closed vet office then, I guessed. The vet must be an avid basketball fan. He probably didn't know Spain would be playing an important game in this championship before agreeing to see me today. I wolfed down my sandwich and turned my back on the bar to finish my beer and to watch the men in the pub still dancing around, euphoric in the victory they vicariously considered theirs.

Someone was waving to me from across the room. The young Spanish guy I'd fucked by the river was there—with a man older than he was, but younger than I was. The companion was a good-looking man. The rent-boy was whispering to the man and both were looking at me and the rent-boy was still waving me over.

He introduced himself as Tome when I went to their table. The older man was introduced as Jose. Tome invited me to join them and help celebrate the EuroBasket victory. I said I couldn't be there long, as I had to find someplace to lodge for the night.

Tome pulled me down at the table and had another round of beers delivered before I could beg off. Jose spoke to me in stilted, but passable, English. I appreciated the effort but was able to understand little more than "Ah, American" and then "nice cock" in another sentence over the din of the celebration in the room. He was an extremely handsome man—lean and elegantly dressed and demeanor—which made the "nice cock" comment all the more surprising, if I'd heard him correctly.

"Tome says me you have very nice cock and fucked him good," he said during a somewhat more quiet break in the surrounding noise. So, I guess I did hear him correctly. I'm not sure that I blush, but if I do, I did. He said it so naturally that I was nonplused and didn't know what to say—so I didn't say anything. It did cause me, though, to take another, assessing, look at him. His complexion was dark and sultry, his hair black and curly—in abundance. Hair curled out from underneath his shirt sleeves and in the cleavage of his shirt front, and his face had one of those perpetual five-o'clock shadows that no amount of shaving was going to get rid of—that he could shave his body in the morning and be hirsute again when he finished at the office. On him, it looked sexy, though.

Images went through my mind of lying next to him, both of us naked and hard, and watching the hair on his body grow before my eyes. Despite laying Tome earlier in the day, I was still horny.

Tome was rubbing Jose's package beneath the top of the table, and after the second round of beers, Tome was rubbing mine as well. I opened the stance of my legs, enjoying the attention, and leaned over and gave Tome a deep kiss.

"I really do have to go find a hotel," I said in slurred words that sounded weak and distant even to me. The third round of beers showed up. "Perhaps you might want to come with me . . . and maybe, too—"

"No problem," Jose was saying. "I have house near here. We fuck; then we sleep. Then maybe we fuck again."

He did have a house, and I was vaguely aware that he had a bedroom in the house when we got there, where, I was to learn, Jose fucked me while I was fucking Tome. I was too buzzed on booze to remember all that went on during the night—other that, indeed, we did fuck, then sleep, then fuck again.

\* \* \* \*

I woke with light streaming through an open window near the head of the double bed. The curtains were streaming in, causing the light to swirl around the room. Lips were on mine, and someone was stroking my hard cock.

Tome.

He was on his belly next to me, an arm laying on my stomach, with the hand encasing my cock. His face was above mine, my arm under him, with my hand on his waist. Tome's right leg was flung over my thighs. His chest was pushed into my side, and I could feel his body shuddering and writhing a bit in a rhythm that had nothing to do with me.

When Tome's lips came off mine and moved down my throat to my nipples, I could see over his head.

Jose.

The older man was suspended over Tome's body, somewhat sideways, and he was doing pushups on Tome's body, fucking him in the ass. Jose was one hirsute dude. On him it looked good—sexy. The curly hair started at the base of his throat, went down over his hard, muscled pecs in swirls and then in a wide swath down lower. I couldn't see down lower, because that was moving and lower than I could see beyond the naked mound of Tome's buttocks.

The man's forearm was covered with curly black hair too. I knew this because he had his fist buried in the mattress right next to my throat. Impulsively, I turned my face to that and licked the hair on his wrist. Seeing that I was awake, he pulled his face over Tome's neck, brought his lips down to mine, and gave me a deep kiss that had me humming.

"Fucked you good last night, didn't I?" he muttered, a silly grin on his face.

"I usually top," I answered.

"That's what you told me last night. So fucking you all the sweeter."

Giving a giggle and an explanation that included something about peeing, Tome struggled out between us and flounced through a door that must have led to a bathroom.

"I want to fuck you again now," Jose said. Without fanfare or request, he was rolling me over on my belly. I certainly got the impression that all questions of what any of us wanted or were willing to do were cleared up the previous night when I was blotto from beer and wine and couldn't

82

remember a thing. Jose was stretched out above me, holding my arms up with a clamp hold on my wrists. I groaned and gave a little woof when his cock entered my ass. But he slid right in. He must have been inside me thickly and for some period of time the previous night—maybe more than once. I moaned and concentrated on surviving and appreciating the ride as he resumed his pushups on my back, pumping me in some sort of pattern in both shallow and deep thrusts.

I felt an arm going under my belly and lifting, coaxing me to come up on my knees, which I did. He was crouched, close over me and lowered his chest onto my back. I sighed at the feel of the silky chest hair sliding on my back. He moved his cock back and forth, side to side in my channel, caressing all of the walls and encouraging me to open as his cock filled out even more. With moans, I did what I could to accommodate him. With a hand on my cheek, he turned my face, and we went into a deep kiss. He was holding me prisoner there, stifling my cries with his tongue, as his hips went into overdrive, pumping me hard, fast, and deep. Riding me hard until my knees buckled and then riding me down flat on the mattress—thrusting, thrusting, thrusting, until we both had come.

Exhausted, I rolled over onto my back, panting and moaning, as Jose stumbled off the bed and went into the bathroom. I heard a shower turn on and then the sounds of Jose fucking Tome in the shower.

This gave me a chance to wonder how I'd gotten here—and where here was. The first was rather obvious. I'd gone to the table in a bar of a guy I'd fucked earlier in the day and let the man he was with buy me beers until I didn't know which way was up. Then this friend had brought us both back to his house and fucked us both silly. I vaguely remembered fucking Tome while Jose was doing me the first time as well. Well, all righty then. I had wanted a good fuck session. This obviously had been one, even if I hadn't been fully conscious to appreciate a lot of it.

And it obviously was going to continue to be one. Tome padded out of the bathroom, toweling himself off. He climbed up on the bed, threw a leg over my stomach, facing away from me, lowered his ass on my hard-again cock, grabbed my knees with his fists, and began to do vigorous butt squats on my cock.

Jose came out of the bathroom, also toweling himself off, laughed, grabbed a camera from the top of a bureau, and started firing off photographs. I wasn't wild about being part of a photo shoot but I was too busy otherwise to raise objections.

Later, sitting at the island in the kitchen as Tome scrambled some eggs, Jose delivered the shock.

"I am town animal doctor. Tome is my assistant. You are very good in bed. Do you live near here?"

The town vet? "Jose," I said. "You're Jose Reis." It came out more as an accusation than a question, and then, when he looked at my quizzically, "My name is Paul. Our mutual friend, Muriel, made an appointment for me to see you yesterday—about getting my stubborn Lab Retriever puppy trained."

"Ah, Muriel," he said. And the way he said it made me wonder if Muriel had set me up again like she had with suggesting the horny Anton and Uxio as construction laborers on my house. They'd done more work on me—with me willing, of course—than they'd done on the house. Had Muriel gauged that I needed extra male attention? If so, I couldn't say that she was wrong.

"Can you help me? Can you train my bitch?"

"How old is puppy?"

I told him, and he told me that my problem was that, until now, it really had been too early for the Lab to concentrate on serious training. "The training should start now," he said.

"Can you do it?"

"I don't train dogs, no. But I can help. Tome here is good at training—at least beginning training."

84

"I don't know if I can bring Mandy all the way here just for regular training."

"No need for you to do that. Tome can come to you for a week."

I wondered what Tome felt about having his week volunteered, but when I looked at him, he was wagging his head—probably wagging his tail too, and the prospect of having him in my house for a week suddenly was appealing to me too.

"After that, you must send dog away for a couple of weeks. I know a great trainer, Monica. She lives in Monforte de Lemos—which is not far from here. But it's far from you, I think."

"I live in Friol, northwest of Lugo."

"Yes, far away. You will have to go there for a week too then when Monica is ready. She will match you to the dog. I call her and make arrangements."

"Could you call her now, please? I should be getting back to Friol. There are men there working on my house."

"No, I don't think so," Jose said, with a smile. "I think there must be a fee for my help and you won't leave yet."

He was so right. I didn't leave for Friol until late in the evening, taking Tome with me. Until then the three of us spent most of the time in Jose's bed, having each other every which way, Tome even had a turn fucking me—although Jose himself never went for a flip-flop—fully satiating my need for sex—well, at least until that night when Tome and I arrived back in Friol.

Mandy was overjoyed to see us. Of course, she was overjoyed to see anyone and fully willing to eat them alive, just as a friendly gesture, of course. Tome impressed me with how fast he was able to stop her from jumping on him. He also impressed me once again in bed that night on how good a blow job he could give.

* * * *

85

I didn't think I would, going into the arrangement with Tome, which had him sleeping in my bed because my bedroom was the only finished bedroom in the Friol house, but I was happy to see him go by the end of his week in residence. This wasn't because he wore me out sexually. It was at least partly because he was rarely there, in my bed. It was like living with Sean all over again—my live-in catting around and giving me short shrift. Tome was almost exactly like Sean. This is what started putting me off on younger men—men in their early twenties. I needed more stability. I think that Tome was when I started writing off just-legal men. I really should have started with Sean.

It wasn't that Tome didn't do his job. He was good with Mandy and she went right to him. I watched them together, and I got some sense of how he brought her under his control. So, when I took him back to Chantada at the end of the week on my way to dropping off Mandy with Monica in Monforte de Lemos for two weeks, I had attained better control over Mandy myself. (That didn't mean that I didn't buy a metal cage for her rather than trust the plastic one.) It's just that I figured most of that out myself. While Tome was good at instructing Mandy, he wasn't good at explaining to me what he was doing and having me try it too.

And he wasn't good about cleaving to me sexually. The worst part was that it was Anton and Uxio all over again as far as bogging down the construction and I wasn't getting the sexual benefit I'd gotten with those two.

When he'd first arrived at work, the middle-aged Alberte had taken one look at me and flipped out a photo packet from his wallet to show me his wife and children. Anton and Uxio had probably talked to him—everyone knew everyone else in this region—but it was obvious to me that he was trying to establish that there would be no hanky-panky between the two of us. Of course, Anton and Uxio had wives and children too, and hanky-panky didn't seem to bother them. The younger, sexier Noé was a bit more flirty, but I think that was more narcissism, impressing himself that he could turn on men as well as women and, to him, a rich American. He and I hadn't gone anywhere yet.

But the first night, when Tome didn't come to bed, I scouted around and found him riding Alberte's cock in the bed of a truck just inside the drive up to the house and, by the third day, I was running across Noé fucking Tome here, there, and everywhere.

Homero was as frustrated by this as I was and was about to fire both of his men, but when he couldn't tell me that neither one of them had not done good work for him, I told him just to let it blow over—as I was doing—and see what the next week after Tome's departure brought.

Tome had not formed any lasting alliances by the end of the week, although he was making money at night beyond Noé and Alberte and beyond my property line, so, when I loaded him and Mandy up in my car, I left a subdued crew working overtime to keep their standing with Homero and Tome just smiling and waving, looking a good bit like Mandy in how he responded to the world.

Mandy was put in her place immediately by Monica when we arrived at the woman's vet and training center in Monforte de Lemos, and I could tell that Mandy was in good hands. I was in good hands too, I could also discern, because for the entire time I was there, talking arrangements, whenever Monica conducted a training element with Mandy, she had me do it too.

"There's a dog show in Santiago in early October," Monica said. "I want you to be there with Mandy."

"I don't think we'll be anywhere close to be competing in a dog show in October," I said, aghast and beginning to sweat.

"No, of course not. But Mandy needs to be acclimated to other dogs and she also needs to start seeing what is going to be expected of her in advanced training."

"Oh, I see. But is it good just to drop her into at a dog show for the first contact with other dogs? I suppose I could take her back to Lugo, where I got her, and see if the man I bought her from still has her siblings to—"

"No, it should be dogs she has no memory of and of other breeds. But I do agree she needs play dates with other dogs before then."

"Play dates? I don't know of any dogs in my area that I could set up play dates with."

"Well, let me think. There is another man in the same stage with his dog. He has recently acquired an English Cocker Spaniel. He's Australian, although he's lived here for some time. His name is Alex. I think I can arrange some dates between your dogs for the week you come to finish off Mandy's training. How does that sound?"

"Fine, I guess, if that's what you recommend."

"It is. I'm sure the two of you will hit it off—it will probably be a good pairing of men as well as dogs. You mentioned you're restoring an old house. Alex inherited one. He might be a big help for you."

As it turned out, Monica didn't know by half how well Alex and I would meld.

# Chapter Six: Alex

Monica had telephoned me to say she had a client with a Labrador puppy that needed to meet other dogs, particularly well-behaved ones. She was obviously interested in chattering on for some time about that dog, my dogs, and the man who owned the dog. But she caught me at a busy time and I quickly began to worry about where the conversation was leading.

"Monica, why are you telling me all this?" I asked. "I am very busy with the B&B, which only opened last week, and the vines—"

"The owner, as I was saying, a very nice man, an American called Paul. He is having trouble restoring an old house. It's in a bad condition. Also, he is in need of more firmness in dealing with his dog, and I know you will give him good advice and set him a good example. He needs to have a break from his house, and his dog needs to meet well-behaved dogs. It will be good for them both, particularly if he spends a few days there with you."

"But the B&B is—"

"Ah, Alex, that is why I am sending him to you. You have the B&B as well as the right temperament for training dogs and teaching owners. And of course you have two very well-behaved playmates for this man's puppy. Mandy is her name. I have told him he must stay with you for two or three days. You have a vacancy for him, I am sure."

I gave up trying to protest. I knew there would be a vacancy and I sighed and resigned myself to doing as Monica wanted. She always seemed to manage to get her way with me. "OK. There will be a room for him. When is he supposed to come here?"

"Tomorrow. I have given him—"

"Tomorrow?" I protested. "But—"

"It's important to me Alex. Are we not friends? And who knows, an American guest may be good for the business. Very good. I am sure he has many friends who are looking for interesting places to visit and who like to drink good wine."

I gave in again. "OK, Monica, I give in. So he arrives tomorrow and is staying for two nights?"

"I think three would be better." Monica said, and I could hear the satisfied smile in her voice.

"All right, three nights." The B&B had only opened three days before, on the Friday, and I knew that it was not full for the coming weekdays. It had been full on the weekend, busy from the first day, busier than I had hoped.

"I will let reception know he is coming. What is his last name?"

I scribbled the details down. Then I remembered his dog was coming also and realized she would also need to be booked in. Dogs were welcome, which was one reason I hoped it would do well, but unless very small and well trained, they were allowed in the foyer and gardens but not allowed to stay in guests' rooms. There were kennels in a converted barn behind the accommodation.

Monica had said the American's puppy was the same age as Figaro, and I wondered again why she was really sending them to me. Monica was the training expert. She was also proud of her reputation as a trainer and jealous of any competition. I certainly wasn't a dog trainer, and if Figaro had always behaved well it was mainly because he had followed Cocky's example. And had classes with Monica.

I had bought Figaro as company for Cocky when the mating I had arranged for her had produced no puppies. I had also now sworn never to have a puppy in the house again. I could not remember Cocky ever being any trouble when she was small but with Edward I had lived a far more contented, fully satisfied, and relaxed life. I also remembered too late that he had refused to have Cocky in the bedroom at night and she had been trained from the start to sleep alone in her bed in the hallway.

Figaro had been spoilt from the beginning, though. As soon as he arrived it was like having a herd of elephants rampaging through the house. His antics were cute, but not all day or after tearing up a packet of toilet rolls and leaving paper scattered from one end of the house to the other. He had somehow unrolled one roll so it stretched all along the main hallway, through several rooms, and around furniture until it ran out. Worse still, the women in the winery office had encouraged him to visit there and it was chaos till I banned him from the business part of the house.

It had been hard but he had learned to sleep in his bed in the hallway eventually and to spend most of the day outside. It was a huge relief that he was now settling down especially as he was still growing and was going to be a big Labrador.

* * * *

As always Enrique arrived on time that night; he, like most Galicians, was very punctual. I was strung out and harassed and hearing his car pull up sent a rush of relief and arousal through me. At last, a break from the demands of business.

As soon as Enrique pulled up I hurried out to meet him, and we barely had time to kiss and embrace before I was pulling him inside.

"Why so eager?" he asked, giving me a half-glad smile and half-questioning look and slipping an arm around my waist as we hurried in.

He was lean and tall, the sort of Spanish man that existed in Galicia and which I found incredibly beautiful. Enrique was a fraction taller than I am, dark haired, and with a short beard or overgrown five-o'clock shadow. He was also very good looking in a purely masculine way, with big, dark bedroom eyes and lips that invited kissing, a body that invited your hands to touch it, and a package that was prominent enough to promise much satisfaction.

There was no time for a drink and talk tonight. I was too tense and in need of release. We went straight to the bedroom, where I pulled him in and kissed him roughly full on the mouth while my hands ran demandingly over his body—his shoulders, his back, squeezing his firm butt cheeks. I grasped his hair and pulled his head in roughly for a deeper kiss before pushing it down so he went onto his knees and unzipped me.

He had nice hands with long, flexible fingers, which now reached in and pulled my hardening cock out and guided it between his lips. I pushed my hips forward, wanting to be buried in his mouth, deep, not played delicately. He took a moment to open up to me and then let me set the rhythm as I roughly stroked in his throat. With a loud grunt, I pulled free and jerked him up and began to strip off his clothes.

He grasped my hands firmly in his. "Careful, Alex, it's from the shop," he said, trying to get me to leave his shirt alone. I understood but didn't care.

"I'll pay for it," I said.

"What is wrong?" he asked, while deftly getting his shirt off over his head before I could tear it off him.

I was faced with a difficult question and his naked chest. I concentrated on his chest. This was not the time to deal with difficult questions. Glossy dark hair curled around his tight, bright nipples, before running down to his bush;

and above that, his face, a look of concern in his eyes. An intimate look that was more than I thought I wanted from him. But inside I felt a small flush that the look was there for me and the feeling went to my cock as I pushed against him, holding him tight, taking his mouth again, but this time firmly and gently, not roughly. Possessing it totally, him opening to me and showing his acceptance of my possession.

I felt his cock growing and pressing against mine through the fabric of his pants. In a few moments those pants fell to the ground and mine joined them, leaving us both naked as neither of us had been wearing briefs.

I pulled him in close again and reached down and held our cocks together, feeling the hardness and heat of him. It was good, very good. This was what I needed. When I couldn't hold off any more I half carried him to the bed lay him on it and climbed up, kneeling over him, a sexy half smile on his face and his eyes slitted. Wanting me to take him. And I did. I knelt between his bent legs and fingered lube into his hole and crowned myself before I pushed his legs back to his shoulders. He had watched me doing it with the same look of fascination and want, and now he could see my face as I entered him.

He always felt tight. His boyfriend was obviously not very thick or didn't fuck him often. I knew they both topped at times. I liked his tightness and strength. He could wrap his legs around me so I could not break free of him and hold me there tight, buried deep, until he was ready to let me go. Years of cycling were paying off for him in bed.

Tonight he arched back once I was inside him, pulling me in deep, and moved with me, moving faster and fucking himself to a rapid ejaculation. Not like him. The first one was always for me. He was not a rent-boy, but I still paid him by paying some of his bills, and he knew he was to be here for me when I wanted him. I was not his first paying lover. I knew he had had several in the last few years and I was sure much of the money he got went to help keep his boyfriend, the musician who had such talent as he told me.

"Sorry," he said, as his breathing settled, but he wrapped his legs about my back and held my cock inside him as he moved in a slow, rolling rhythm, making this one for me. He massaged me with his channel as I moved with him and looked into his eyes, having no idea what I saw there and, for now, not caring. I fucked him longer than I had expected before I came, at last taken away from the irritations of the day.

I rolled off him to lay along his side and wrapped an arm about his neck. "So, what is wrong," I asked him, looking at the ceiling, torn between wanting a no-strings fuck and knowing all was not well with him.

I liked him. He managed one of the best men's clothing shops in Lugo and somehow we had connected a couple of months before. Me looking for a new "regular," after the last one began to show signs of serious drug use, and him looking for a new sugar daddy.

"Luis has only been home twice in the last week," he said. I heard a catch in his voice and pulled his face in for a kiss. Then I turned and wrapped my arms and legs around him.

I had heard that his musician boyfriend, Luis, slept around with women as well as men, but I knew what he and Enrique had was strong. Love is strange, and Enrique had seemed content with Luis—worshiping him.

"He left with most of his clothes last time. I was not there but when I got home—"

"Shhh," I said covering his mouth again and taking his cock in my hand and stroking it, glad when he began to stiffen and returned the kissing and reached for me.

I knew there was something I had to do if I cared for him. And I did care for him.

"I want you to stay the night."

He began to lick over my neck, pausing to dip his tongue lightly into my ear, which sent an intense shiver along my spine and to my core, before moving it to my chest and on down. I had said it right.

In the morning he had breakfast with me before I saw him off. At his car I kissed him on the lips and said, "If you want the job of managing the B&B, it's yours. You can come back this evening to discuss it. And stay the night, if you want." We kissed again, his eyes sparkling, and he reached out and grasped my hand.

As he drove off I was pleased I had said what I had to him. He was an excellent customer person, and I knew he wanted a change that would open more opportunities for him. Managing the B&B, which was almost a three-star hotel, would open a lot of opportunities for him. And now the business was operating and doing better than expected, I knew I had to have more help.

As for him and me. I liked him. I knew he could be committed and probably monogamous. I knew he looked terrific, was good in bed, and behaved well in public at social events, and he knew almost everyone who was anyone in Galicia. I had held back on letting myself have feelings for him because of Luis, but if I could let go . . . I felt a surge of pleasure run through me. He was delicious.

* * * *

All I knew about the man I was expecting that Tuesday morning at ten o'clock was his name, Paul; that he was an American; and that his dog was a Labrador bitch called Mandy.

I had called Monica back, asking her to send Paul straight to the B&B reception. They had instructions to call me when he arrived. I was edgy. It was a new day and the difficult questions were back. And what had seemed clear in the early morning afterglow of sex now seemed rash. Enrique might have excellent customer service skills but running a large B&B with a restaurant was not the same as managing an upmarket clothing shop. I knew, though, that I had put off hiring a permanent manager, even though I had interviewed several people for the job, as not long after

95

meeting him Enrique had been at the back of my mind for the position. Also none of the applicants had been ideal.

Not only was the B&B demanding my time, Vendimia, the grape harvest, was only a couple of weeks away. After seeing Enrique off, I had been out to check the vines, still all the Mencia variety, as I did each morning at this time of year, and when I met up with Pepe in the vineyard he had suggested it was time to trim back the excess vine growth in preparation for the harvest. I had agreed. Many vineyards didn't trim, because it was labor intensive, but Edward had liked to follow the old ways, and trimming the vines back a week or two before picking gave the grapes a boost in the last weeks and made harvesting them much easier. Our wines were very high quality and I had no doubt the care we took of the vines was important.

When I returned to the house, ten o'clock had been and gone and there had been no call to say the American had arrived. But I knew that foreigners often got lost trying to find us, even though there were signs pointing in the direction of the B&B at the major crossroads. GPS, unfortunately, was very unreliable in Galicia and particularly so in the Ribeira Sacra region we were in. I headed to the office to do paperwork, hoping the American might not come after all.

But the American did arrive, brought to the house by an annoyed Jacobo. Paul was looking rather muddy and embarrassed and trying to apologize as Jacobo informed me that the American's dog, Mandy, was locked in a barn because she had been caught chasing the chickens and Paul had slipped in the mud trying to catch her. She had apparently leaped out of Paul's car window when they were passing the house barn and she saw the chickens. I wanted to laugh as Jacobo described what had happened next. The scene of him and Paul chasing Mandy as she galloped about after the chickens, having quickly discovered there was more than one and that chasing half a dozen chickens was an even better game than chasing one. Then Paul had slipped and

96

fallen in the mud by the water trough and been lucky not to hit his head on the stone edge. Jacobo had been torn between helping him and getting Mandy before she got the chickens. Fortunately, just then, Mandy had noticed Paul was lying on the ground and had stopped to wonder why and Jacobo had got hold of her collar.

Paul was looking bruised as well as muddy and obviously needed to get cleaned up. I had stopped myself, with difficulty, from laughing at the story as I was not sure the American would take it well if I did, perhaps thinking I was laughing at him and his predicament.

"At least you found the place," I said, offering him my hand, which he waved away as he had mud on his. "No problem, all mud is good in Galicia," I reassured him, and grabbed for his hand and shook it. His grip became firm once I had shown I was serious.

"Jacobo will take you and your car to the B&B, where you can wash the mud off and get cleaned up."

"I am sorry about the chickens and happy to pay for any that—"

I waved the suggestion away. "No problem," I assured him. "Come back here at two for lunch, and then we can discuss the dogs. I will take care of Mandy and get her to the kennels at the B&B for you."

"Thank you," he said, giving me a grateful smile that showed him to be an attractive man under the mud. "It was not easy to find you, even with the coordinates in the GPS," Paul added, as he left.

I had no idea what I had expected Paul to be like, but I was pleasantly surprised to find he was a well-maintained, good-looking man, with a mild, well-educated American accent. A TV accent, I called it. I admit that strong American accents often put me off. He reminded me of Edward in some way, and I was humming as I trotted down the steps out of the house and across to the barn, where Jacobo has said he had locked Mandy up. She could have accompanied

97

them to the B&B, but I wanted to get a look at this devil dog without Paul about.

I was also now wondering if Monica had an ulterior motive in sending Paul and Mandy to me. I laughed and then frowned. I had only just met the man, and he had come here to get his dog used to other dogs, and only that morning I had been thinking of something permanent with Enrique. I shook my head. I did not need even more problems.

When I opened the barn door a ball of energy bounded at me, almost knocking me over; but not with aggression. Mandy wanted to lick me to death in her relief at being released from her prison. I managed to grab her collar and attach the lead I had brought before she saw anything more interesting in the distance and got away from me.

Well, she certainly loved people. But she took several minutes to settle down to being walked on the lead, and even when she had she wanted to sniff and explore everything interesting that we passed, and it took quite a bit of strength to pull her back to walking beside me. I had a premonition that in her present state she might be more of a bad influence on my dogs than they could be a good influence on her. Paul had a lot of work to do with her before I was letting them get together for more than a brief supervised play. Figaro, in particular, would be very easily and very happily led astray by her.

I would have to discuss a plan for the dogs with Paul over lunch and wondered how I could put my desire to keep them apart as much as possible diplomatically, so as not to hurt his feelings. Mandy gave every sign of being Paul's spoiled "child" and the apple of his eye.

# Chapter Seven: Paul

"I just noticed that the trees are beginning to turn color."

"Yes, they do that every year—like they do where you say you come from in the States. Not so much where I came from in Australia, though. The scenery here isn't anything like where I came from in Australia—thank God. More wine?"

"Yes, please," I answered, holding my glass out for Alex to refill from a jug. It hadn't even made it into the bottle yet. I knew this jug full never would make it to the bottle. This was the way wine was meant to be drunk—and available—I thought, grown in the fields—fincas, he called them—on the slope down to the river from here and made into wine on the premises. We were on the terrace of his rambling home—now part of a large B&B—stretched out on chaise lounges in robes and looking down at the River Mino as the sun set.

There weren't any other guests of the B&B out on the terrace—thank the gods, as, other than the robes, which Alex had supplied, we were both in the altogether. The other guests were all at dinner in the dining room, which opened out onto the stone terrace down the line of the house's stone wall a good distance. The light from the French windows shone on the terrace tiles, although Alex and I, increasingly, were in the shadows. There also was the tinkle of silverware and the crystal as well as the buzz of light laughter and conversation. I noticed just then that we could hear the background music, as well. A Spanish guitar playing a classical tune—a familiar one.

"Your thoughts? Regrets?" Alex asked in a low voice.

"No, no regrets. Of course not. I had just noticed the music," I answered.

"A local artist. Xavier Franco."

I laughed.

"You know of him?" Alex asked.

"Yes, I knew him once. Very well. Biblically even." My mind went back to the Galician guitarist I'd met and guided on his tour around the States what seemed like a lifetime ago—the reason why I had come to Spain. I was pleased that I could laugh about it now. For the longest time I couldn't laugh about Xavier.

"Ah," was all Alex said. We could openly refer to that now—my preferences, his preferences, within the last couple of hours our shared preferences. I had been here, at his B&B, for the last two weeks. It was supposed to have been only for two or three days, a play date between our dogs, arranged by Monica, a mutual acquaintance. But I'd been here for two weeks and our dogs had yet to play together. We'd played together now, though, Alex and I, but only just now—so far. Who knew whether it would go anywhere from here? We were both older. We'd both professed to like younger men. And then we'd fallen into each other's arms.

We'd waltzed around each other for the two weeks, each of us knowing the preference of the other, increasingly interested in each other, but only now, when I was preparing to go back to renovating my own home in Friol, some distance from here, had we taken the step—made the leap, dived into the abyss. We had just fallen on each other in his bedroom, just inside the French windows from here. One minute we were civilized men discussing the jug of wine he'd just brought to be tasted before I left to return to Friol, and the next we were rutting animals. We'd struggled clumsily, not knowing who was to do what to whom and winding up

100

doing each other in turn, first me fucking Alex and then Alex fucking me, slowly, languidly, completely.

"So, if your trees change color here, how many seasons do you have in Galicia?" I didn't want to think about Xavier just now—or all of the young Spanish men I'd fucked in this season in Galicia. I wanted to fuck Alex again, and be fucked by Alex. I didn't know what he thought, though. I was afraid of knowing what he thought.

"Four, like everyone else," Alex asked, with a laugh. "Top up the wine glass for you?"

"Yes, please. I mean, how many distinct seasons?"

"Four. It can get cold as a witch's tit here in the winter. And the wind coming off the river valley . . . whooie. But the best is yet to come," he blurted out after a pause, turning to look directly at me, his scrutinizing gaze running down my body. I suddenly felt deficient, old, and I instinctively sucked in my stomach—the stomach that both of his hands had run down as I was spooned into his belly, one hand wrapping itself around my cock and the other working its fingers into my passage, finding and stroking my prostate until I ejaculated for him and, with little adjustment, he penetrated me from behind and began to stroke between the fingers he was using to stretch my channel to help me accommodate him.

"The best season?" I asked, my voice a bit shaky from the memory of him inside me.

"Yes. I think the autumn is the best season here—colorful, with crisp mornings and sun-burnished afternoons."

He reached over, across the short distance between our lounge beds, ran his hand into the folds of my borrowed robe—his robe, with the scent of him on it—possessed my cock, and slow stroked me as we continued to talk as if nothing was happening between us. I sighed, turned slightly toward him and away from the sounds in the dining room, raising and bending my left leg, creating a wall between us and the rest of the house. The folds of the robe fell away, so we both could see my hard cock with his hand on it. He brushed his robe open as well, and took possession of himself with his other hand. He was stroking us both to the same slow rhythm.

"Good. I would have missed having four distinct seasons," I answered, trying to keep my voice in check.

"How long have you been here now—in Galicia?" he asked. "I guess I never asked you that. Monica didn't tell me, either. She just said you had a sweet, but wild, Lab that you couldn't control but wanted to keep."

"Just three months. Just one season. A season in Galicia. It seems like a whole different lifetime."

"But you're asking about the seasons here. Does that mean you've decided to stay in Galicia."

"Yeah, I'm staying."

"I mean because you haven't been sure. You've mentioned a couple of times how hard it's been to renovate your house in Friol and how your former firm has been after you to return to Washington."

"I've decided to stay. Mandy's under control now. I couldn't leave her and it would be too much of a hassle to get her into the States." That was true, of course—not just the hassle, but that I couldn't leave my precious Lab now. Alex had thrown up his hands when we'd arrived, discovering how wild and untamed—and exuberant—Mandy had been. He'd flatly said he couldn't expose his two dogs to her for fear they'd go wild too, rather than help tame Mandy. His vineyard manager, Jacobo, had been the savior. He'd taken Mandy to his cottage. He said I'd have to leave her to him, though, and not visit her for a week or more or I'd let her slide. In the meantime I should spend time with Alex' two dogs to learn from them what I should expect from a well-behaved Mandy.

He said he wouldn't be cruel to Mandy but he'd be firm—that he'd give her what she needed. And he'd been good to his word. She was reasonably responsive now. I'd worked with her with Alex and Jacobo the last three days. We were getting there. Still, Alex had said I'd have to work with her a couple of more weeks all on my own before we could put her in with his two dogs. And Monica had said all three dogs had to be ready for an October show—that they had to be good with each other by then. So, I was taking her back to Friol so we could work without distractions.

And speaking of distractions, Alex' hand job was driving me to distraction. I reached down again to brush him away, but he growled, "No, I am in command now. You will come for me," and, with a sigh, I relaxed, happy to submit to him. I too needed to learn to take commands, I realized.

I'd thought, no problem with the plan that had been laid out for Mandy and me. I'd take Mandy back to Friol for a couple of weeks. I had to check on how the house renovations there were going anyway. And then I'd bring her back for what was supposed to be that three-day play date with Alex' dogs. And then that would be that. Back home to Friol.

But now I'd slept with Alex. Now I wasn't at all sure "that could be that." But maybe Alex hadn't been affected by being with me in the same way that I had been affected by being with him. Maybe . . . and then, when I was nearly ready to ejaculate, Alex took his hand away.

"As long as you're thinking of staying," he then murmured, "and because I know you've mentioned a few times about being at loose ends without much to do—I wondered if you might be interested in taking on the management of the B&B. I think I'm going to have my hands full with the winery for at least a couple of years."

"Manage the B&B?" I asked. "What do I know about managing a B&B?"

"As much as I knew about managing a vineyard when Edward brought me here." Alex replied.

"That would mean I'd have to live here. Friol is too far away to commute."

"Yes, there's that. You could rent your place out for a couple of years, of course," Alex said. I looked over at him. He wasn't looking at me; he had his eyes cast down toward the river—or where the river, I knew, was, although night had fallen and I couldn't see it. I could see dottings of lights across the river, though—of what I knew were other picturesque stone villages and houses with other steep terraces and small fields planted to grapes. God, this was a beautiful country.

"I thought you'd found your manager," I said. "I thought the young man—your friend who manages the clothing store in Lugo—was going to manage the B&B. Enrique." I, in fact, thought Enrique was more in the picture with Alex than that. They were lovers. That was a serious complication for me. I didn't like to share. There was nothing but grief to be had from that.

"Enrique turned me down. Well, he said he might be interested if he only did the customer service and front desk operation. He didn't want to take on the whole job. But he's back with his boyfriend and his boyfriend has moved all his things back in with him and didn't want to move from Lugo."

"His boyfriend?"

"Yes, well. I think the boyfriend is going to be the spanner in the works for any chance of Enrique moving here to work. Theirs is an on-again, off-again relationship. No stability, but no telling where it will go or if either one will realize it when it's gone. I'm too old to wait that out. So, I'm looking again. For a manager. For someone to manage the B&B."

"And to live somewhere nearby, I suppose."

"Yes. Nearby," Alex said. Then he laughed, and turned his eyes on me. There was enough light for me to know that, despite the laugh, there was an intensity in his eyes. And a hint of longing—a touch of worry and fear even. Could it be that he was as concerned about what was developing here as I was? "For the right person, it could be here, right there, through the glass doors."

"Your bedroom?" I asked.

"Is that what's through those doors?" Alex turned and looked back at the building. "Why, so it is."

"It's a proposal to think about," I answered.

"While you're thinking, would it help to have another look at the accommodations that go with the position? The bed, for instance?"

"What, now?"

"Yes, now. I haven't finished with you. I said you would come for me again and I meant it. And then maybe at dawn again to see and experience it together in partial light—and then later in the morning in full light."

"Yes, I think that's a sterling idea," I said, sitting up on the side of the chaise lounge, facing Alex. He sat up as well and reached over, cupping the back of my head, gently pulling my face to his, and taking my lips in a long, deep kiss. His other hand went to my cock. I hadn't lost the erection he'd already given me.

"Shall we bring the wine in with us?" he asked when he'd released my lips—but not my cock.

"Wine? In bed? I don't think that would be wise. And I don't really want to be any more drunk than I am now for the next couple of hours."

"You haven't had that much wine."

"It's not just the wine I'm drunk on. Who's on top first?"

"Let's wrestle for it—on the bed," he whispered as he rose up on his elbow and looked at me intensely.

"About the wine . . . ," I whispered.

"Good point," he said, as he slid over onto the lounge bed I was on, turned me belly to the mattress, pulled my robe away while covering us both with his, penetrated me deep with his cock, and held me close, only his pelvis and my buttocks moving, as he fucked me to heaven once more.

~

105

# About the Authors

**Shabbu** is the combined pen name for two established authors, one on the East Coast of the United States, and an Australian, until recently living on the East Coast of Australia, but now in southern Europe, who spin erotica together in cyber space.

**Habu,** a bisexual former supersonic spy jet pilot, intelligence agent, and diplomat, is a published mainstream novelist and short story writer under another name and in another dimension of his life.

**Sabb,** once an accountant and sometime property developer, is a wild barbarian at heart, who knows that love is out there of you're lucky enough to find it.

You can find habu and Sabb at BarbarianSpy.com. These authors' erotic, and nonerotic, e-novels and anthologies are published by BarbarianSpy in e-book and paperback, and available from all major on-line book retailers.

Our authors like to receive feedback and to have reviews of their work posted at distributor and review sites.

## BarbarianSpy
### FOR LITERARY HEAT

**Not all books listed below may currently be on release.**
\* indicates the book is available in paperback and e-book.

### BOOKS BY CHRIS CROSS
**Multisexual Adult Romance**
Pulaski Square
Chocolate in Vanilla (MF)
Christmas with Chris (MMF) (MM) (MF)

### BOOKS BY ALEX LOCKHEED
**Transgender Romance**
Meeting Jenna
**Transgender Other**
Being Sarah

### BOOKS BY DIRK HESSIAN
**Xtreme Historical Erotica**
Dirk's Ancient Times Collection (Print only Bundle)\*
The King's Men
Shores of Tripoli\*
Prophecy of Noto
Pretender's Fate

**General Historical Erotic Romance**
Dirk's America's Founding Collection (Print only Bundle)\*
Soldier,Spy
Ridden West
Deliver a Virgin
Clouds and Rain
Confederate Gold
Puttin on the Ritz
To the Hessian Hills
Fire Down the Valley\*
Constantinople\*
The Beautiful Way\*
Blue and Gray
Colonel's Treasure
Beginning of Time
Labyrinth

## BOOKS BY HABU
**Gay Erotica**
**Memoir Faction**
Flying High, Diving Deep*
**Xtreme Erotica**
Fist of Gold
Liaisons
Chain Gang Banged (Short Story)
Tramp Steaming*
Escape to Girne
Silas' Choice*
Last Call
Choke Hold
Apyko: The Greek Pimp
Visits of the Schlange
Second Coming: Emile La Cour Unleashed*
Vortex: Sacrificed by Curiosity*
Dark Angel Sounding *(in e-book & included in Sounding:Ultimate Control paperback)*
Sounding: Ultimate Control *(Print Only)*
Sounding Five *(in e-book & included in Sounding:Ultimate Control paperback)*
**Romance**
Key Westing (short)
Finding a New Sam
Bangkok Summer Seduction
The Photograph
Inevitable Case
Turn to Love
Rain Check
Built for Pleasure (Sci Fi)
Danny's Choice*
Pull of the Groove
Sugar n Spice Christmas
Friday Nights with Lenny (Christmas Romance)
Snowy, Snowy Nights (Christmas Romance)
Tank n Bull
Sail to the Sun
War Letters
Ravens Roost
Caribbean Cruise Top to Bottom
Arena Stage

Trading Partners (Valentine's Day)
Four Coins
Lower Than the Heart (Valentine's Day)
Brambleton
Gotta Keep Trying
Finding Amnad
Platres Conclave
**Other Novels/Novellas**
Ranger Guided
Key Westing
Syrian Ram
Temptation's Clutches*
Descent into Chaos
Escape to Girne
Journey Through Abilene
Harmony and Dissonance
Stallion Station
Racing With the Devil (espionage suspense)
Prepared in Cape Verdi
Gilded Cage
House on Park*
Anything for Ambition
Dance of the Ravishers
Hard Knocks U*
My Neighbor's Spa*
Man's Man: Tales of a High Priced Gay Hooker*
Trip Money
The Indian Doctor
Sailorboy
Home to Fire Island
**Murder Mysteries**
All Fools Day Foolery (Mike Kavanagh)
Inevitable Case (Mike Kavanagh)
Vanishing Laura
Death on a Ping Pong Table
Clint Folsom Mysteries Compendium Volume 1*
Death to Blonds - Stolen Judgment (Clint Folsom Mystery)*
Clint Folsom Mysteries Compendium Volume 2*
**Gay Erotica Anthologies**
Earth Cry*
Shunga
Habu's Christmas Balls

Eight in D*
DevilMENt
Silas' Choices*
Stallion Station (A Novella in Parts)
Eleven to the Dogs*
Fifty Seventy*
Spy Tails 001*
Spy Tails 002*
Doubled*
Doubled Again*
Tails in the Tropics*
Tails in the Med*
Tails in the West*
Rough Riders*
Grab Bag 1*
Grab Bag 2*
Grab Bag 3*
Grab Bag 4*
Grab Bag 5*
Grab Bag 6*
Grab Bag 7*
Grab Bag 8*
Grab Bag 9*
Beyond the Beaded Curtain*
Habu's Christmas Balls
The Sporting Life*
Fetish Galore!*
**Literary Gay Erotica**
Cairo Surrender*
The Handyman*
Homeward Bound
Journey to Mirage*
**Bisexual/Menage/Multisexual Erotica**
And Eat it Too
Two Men, One Woman*
Every Which Way
Summer of Denial
Death on a Ping Pong Table
Cruising Gigolo
13 Ways for Halloween
Luther*
The Indian Prince*

## BOOKS BY SABB
Driver Reliever
Hiring in Hollywood
The Legend of Holleystone Grange
Surprise Encounters*
She is He
Wrong Man
Loyal to his King
Barbarian Tales - Book One - Traveler's Tales*
Barbarian Tales - Book Two - Journeys Begin*
Barbarian Tales - Book Three - The Inheritance*
Barbarian Tales - Book Four - Road to Persepolis*

## BOOKS BY SHABBU
A Season in Galicia
Blind Dates*
Velvet Interrogation
Finding Jason
Dirty Pool
Operation Black Jade
Cigars!*
Angel in the Barn
Gayly Complicated*
Despoiling David
The Tree of Idleness*
I Met a Man
Rough Road to Happiness

## BOOKS BY STEPHEN KESSEL
**Gay Romance**
The Forever Man
Two Chances

## BOOKS BY KIM BLACK
**Lesbian Romance**
Transfixed on Tammie (F/T lesbian)